So who was

Cole opened his e[...] quickly shut them [...] *never* bedded redheads. They reminded him too much of his father and—

And then he remembered everything.

Jolie Tanner. *The* Jolie Tanner.

Hated since childhood for the sins of her mother.

Avoided ever since for sins that were all her own.

Wanted...

Cole's body certainly thought so.

Wanted for quite some time now if he were being brutally honest...but only in the sense of a spoiled child wanting the one thing his parents had denied him.

So he'd been attracted to her? So what? Most men were.

He'd never followed through.

And then Jolie moved in her sleep, and he groaned aloud and brought a hand up through her hair, presumably to persuade her to rearrange her body elsewhere.

Except that his hand stayed right where it was and so did she.

KELLY HUNTER Accidentally educated in the sciences, Kelly Hunter has always had a weakness for fairy tales, fantasy worlds and losing herself in a good book. Husband? Yes. Children? Two boys. Cooking and cleaning? Sigh. Sports? No, not really—in spite of the best efforts of her family. Gardening? Yes. Roses? Of course. Kelly was born in Australia and has traveled extensively. Although she enjoys living and working in different parts of the world, she still calls Australia home.

Kelly's novels *Sleeping Partner* and *Revealed: A Prince and a Pregnancy* were both finalists for the Romance Writers of America RITA® Award in the Best Contemporary Series Romance category!

Visit Kelly online at www.kellyhunter.net.

THE MAN SHE
LOVES TO HATE

KELLY HUNTER

~ Dirty Filthy Money ~

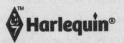

TORONTO NEW YORK LONDON
AMSTERDAM PARIS SYDNEY HAMBURG
STOCKHOLM ATHENS TOKYO MILAN MADRID
PRAGUE WARSAW BUDAPEST AUCKLAND

Recycling programs
for this product may
not exist in your area.

ISBN-13: 978-0-373-52827-1

THE MAN SHE LOVES TO HATE

First North American Publication 2011

Copyright © 2011 by Kelly Hunter

THE MAN SHE
LOVES TO HATE

"The truth is rarely pure and never simple."
—*The Importance of Being Earnest*
by Oscar Wilde

PROLOGUE

'HANNAH, wait up!' Jolie Tanner slipped out of her house yard and slammed the wire gate shut behind her as she raced to catch up with her friend. Usually Hannah called out on the way past, or Jolie waited on the step for her—the plan wasn't foolproof but they'd been walking to school together since kindergarten and, unless one of them was sick, they had the routine down pat. 'Han!'

But Hannah didn't slow down or turn around. Hannah kept right on walking.

Cole walked with Hannah today and that was unusual. Cole was Hannah's big brother. Big as in seventeen years old and tall and strong and in his final year of high school. Big as in handsome, and popular, and good at absolutely everything.

Cole had shaggy black hair, olive skin, and green *green* eyes framed by dark curling lashes. Cole left every Hollywood teen heart-throb for dead. Including the vampires.

Hannah adored her brother. Jolie adored him too, although Jolie's adoration of late had been tinged with an awareness she couldn't describe. She'd begun to feel tongue-tied around him. She didn't know where to look or what to do. Hannah had noticed. Hannah had started teasing Jolie about her stupid reactions to Cole.

Was *that* why Hannah wouldn't turn around?

Because Jolie *knew* Cole was too old for her, too everything for her, and that he would never look at her like *that*. It was just a phase she was going through. That was what her mother had said when Jolie had mentioned—kind of—that she got clumsy around Cole Rees these days. Rachel Tanner had smiled her crinkly smile and told Jolie she'd grow out of it eventually.

Her total crush on Cole Rees was nothing to worry about. It was *just a phase*.

'Hannah, wait up.' Slinging her bag more securely over her shoulder, Jolie began to run to catch up.

'Just keep walking,' said Cole.

'But what do I say?' asked Hannah, her eyes stricken and her expression piteous. 'Cole, she's my best friend. What do I *say?*'

'Nothing.'

'Do you think she knows?'

'How would *I* know?' Cole Rees didn't know anything any more. He'd thought his parents' marriage was solid. Not great, but solid. He'd thought his father walked on water. Reality had come as a shock. His father had been having an affair—for over a year now he'd been having an affair. With Jolie Tanner's mother. His father had admitted it last night in a blazing row. His father wanted a divorce. Cole and Hannah had been upstairs but they'd heard it all. The accusations, the acknowledgement, and then the tears.

So many tears.

Jolie called out again, and Cole kept right on walking.

Little Jolie T might have been just a kid but she was already a beauty. Hair the colours of firelight and big grey eyes that seemed to see everything. Jolie's mother was one of the most beautiful women Cole had ever seen. Jolie would be the same. Just give her time.

And then Jolie was beside them on the footpath, those big grey eyes bright and her red ponytail bouncing. 'Hannah, did you do the homework for the test?'

Hannah said nothing. Hannah shot him another pleading glance and Cole wished himself somewhere, anywhere, else.

Jolie had been in and out of their home since she'd been tiny. She wasn't family but she was a part of Cole's life—a part that he'd taken for granted and been used to. Hannah's friend. Quirky. Funny. Always scribbling in a little notebook she never would show anyone. Cole had asked Hannah what was in it once. Pictures, Hannah had said, so he'd then had to ask the obvious. What kind of pictures?

All kinds, had been Hannah's reply. Animals, people, colour. She drew everything.

Cole had found the notion oddly fascinating.

'Han,' whispered Jolie again, bringing Cole back to the present with a scowl. 'Did you do your homework?'

Hannah shook her head to signify no, and then just put her head down and kept right on walking. Not a lot of homework happening in the Rees household last night.

Cole glanced at Jolie and saw the puzzled hurt in her eyes. Grimly he put his own head down and kept walking. Quickly. Silently. Trying to pretend that little Jolie Tanner wasn't hurrying along beside them, trying to keep up with them, and wondering what on earth was going on.

That was the way the three of them walked to school.

Cole hated every step of it.

Something was wrong. Dreadfully wrong. Hannah wouldn't talk to her, Cole had ignored her. Cole had disappeared once they'd reached the school buildings. Jolie had been hoping that once he'd gone, she might have more to say.

But Hannah wouldn't even look at her.

'Hannah, what is it?' asked Jolie. 'Say something.'

'I can't be your friend any more,' she said in a choked voice, and Jolie looked closer. She was crying.

'What?' Jolie's heartbeat tripled. 'Hannah, what are you talking about?'

But Hannah had fled then, to the classroom, and by recess Sarah wasn't talking to Jolie, either.

By lunchtime, not one of the girls Jolie and Hannah usually hung out with were talking to Jolie, and Jolie was beside herself. She went looking for Cole, and finally found him coming out of the library alone. He saw her. He tried to walk straight past her.

'Cole,' she said, scrambling to keep up with him. 'Cole, there's something wrong with Hannah. She won't talk to me. She's crying. Cole, she's so upset. What's going on?' Jolie put her hand to his arm to slow him down and gasped as he wrenched violently out of her reach. 'Please... I... I just want to know what's wrong?'

'Ask your mother,' he said, and his voice sounded harsh and defensive. 'And don't *touch* me.'

Jolie blushed scarlet and put the offending hand behind her back. 'I won't touch. I'm sorry. I didn't mean to.' And when he stared at her with burning green eyes, 'Cole, please. I just... Hannah hates me and I don't know why,' she pleaded. 'Hannah, and Sarah, and now Evie and Bree too. No one will even *talk* to me.'

'Why should I care?' he said finally. 'Why should I give a *damn* about you and your problems? Just stay away from Hannah and stay the hell away from me.'

'But why?' she whispered, fighting the urge to flee. 'Cole, I don't know what's wrong. Cole, please.' She didn't know how else to phrase her question. 'What have I done *wrong*?'

CHAPTER ONE

Ten Years Later

JOLIE TANNER might as well have been carrying a dead body as far as level of difficulty was concerned. But there was nothing else for it, so she hauled and she shoved until finally the box was on the ski sled and strapped into place. So what if cardboard packing boxes weren't meant to endure such treatment? This one didn't have a choice.

Time to go. Past time to go, but Jolie turned back towards the cabin, her rubber-soled snow boots scrabbling for purchase on the icy step as she pulled the door closed and locked it. Everything was as it should be inside the cabin. Clean, tidy and utterly impersonal. Mission complete.

Climbing into the ski mobile's driver's seat, Jolie headed for the gondola next and went through the process of getting the box off the sled and into the waiting ski gondola, grimacing as the box took yet another beating for her efforts. From there she headed for the ski field control tower and parked the ski mobile in its spot beside the door.

The ski mobile rig was Hare's. So too was the heavy

coat he'd insisted Jolie put on before he let her head for
the cottage. The two-way radio in her pocket was his
too. It had crackled to life a few minutes ago with Hare
in his official capacity of ski-field manager telling her
to make swift with the time because the weather was
getting worse, the last gondola ride down mountain was
leaving five minutes ago, and she'd damn well better be
on it.

Everything in its place, she unhitched the sled and
stored it in the lock-up. *Everything in its place*—a
little phrase Hare rammed home to every employee on
the mountain. Everything where it ought to be or you
could get the hell off Silverlake Mountain and go down
and work the bars and restaurants and ski lodges of
Queenstown instead.

'Is it done?' Hare murmured as she slipped into the
control room and shut the door behind her.

'It's done.' Jolie set the ski mobile keys on the key
rack by the door, and the two-way back in its charger
on the counter. She pulled the cottage keys from her
pocket and held them out towards Hare. These ones had
no hanging spot that Jolie knew of. 'Mama said to give
you these, as well.'

When Hare rubbed at one of his arms rather than take
them, Jolie set the keys down on the counter. Frankly,
she never wanted to lay eyes on them again. She could
hardly blame Hare for wanting the same.

'Never did sit right with me, that arrangement,' muttered Hare.

'Yeah, well, you're not exactly in the minority.' A
truth for a truth and only for Hare. Everyone else got
defiant and hostile silence—a defence mechanism that
predated her teens. 'But it's done with now.'

Death had a way of finalising things.

'How's your mama holding up?' asked the big man. 'She at the funeral?'

'No,' said Jolie wearily. 'Of course she's not. She was heading out to walk alongside Lake Wanaka for a while instead. Reckons she'll say goodbye to him there.'

'She working the bar this evening?' asked Hare and Jolie nodded.

'Yes. You're invited to come down and drink to the dead tonight, by the way. Discreetly, of course, but it's on the house. It's the wake you have when you're not having a wake.'

'She loved him,' said Hare gruffly. 'You give her that, if nothing else.'

'I know. It's just—' Bitterness didn't become her; Jolie tried her best to avoid it. But she'd just spent an afternoon removing all traces of her mother from James Rees's self-indulgent life and remembering in the process exactly how much her mother had given up for him and what she'd received in return. 'I know.'

Not Hare's fault, Jolie's foul mood. Not his fault that he'd been the unlucky employee charged with running herd on young Jolie that first time Rachel Elizabeth Tanner had gone up to the high cabin to be with her married lover. Not Hare's fault he'd been stuck with Jolie every time after that until Jolie had deemed herself old enough to not need a babysitter any more.

Hare had taught her to ski, taught her the mountain and kept her safe from everything but bitter reality.

Nothing could keep her safe from that.

Things had changed for Jolie after James Rees's affair with Rachel Tanner had come to light. Jolie's friends had not remained friends and she'd never really got the hang of making new ones. And when the boys had started to notice Jolie—and they had—Jolie had discovered that former friends could turn into jealous and angry enemies who knew exactly where to hit so as to make the hurt go in deep.

'You gonna stick around Queenstown for a while?' asked Hare. 'Help your mama adjust?'

Jolie shrugged. 'I can stay a couple of weeks. Then I'll have to get back to work in Christchurch.'

'Heard you landed a drawing job there.'

'I did.' Sheer bloody-mindedness and talent had got her a job as a graphic artist for a film special effects company. Sheer bloody-mindedness and talent kept her there. The pay-off being that she didn't have to deal with reality on a daily basis. Reality was overrated.

'Could you do it from here?'

'Why would I want to do that?'

'I don't know.' Hare seemed to hesitate. He scratched his head and pulled a frown. 'Might be different for you here now that James is gone.'

'I can't see why. Hannah's still here. Cole's still here. James's widow is here.' The reclusive Christina Rees. 'And they still own half the town. They've *never* been inclined to make anything easy for a Tanner.'

'Wasn't easy for any of you,' said Hare gruffly. 'Could be a good time to let go of old grudges.'

'Now you're being rational,' said Jolie. 'Interaction between Tanners and Reeses is never rational.'

'Doesn't have to be that way,' said Hare.

'Yeah, it does,' she said softly, and opened up to Hare because the big man had always been kind to her and knew more of the real Jolie Tanner than most. 'Hare, I don't want to come back to Queenstown. All I ever did here was hide myself away from other people. Put on masks so that people would see what they expected to see. A young girl completely at home in a bar full of strangers. The defiant daughter of James Rees's mistress. A siren in my own right, fully comfortable in the role. All of them masks, whereas in Christchurch...' Jolie shrugged awkwardly. 'I've finally gathered the courage to step out from behind the masks and just be me. I kind of like being me.'

'You're making friends, then?'

'Not quite.' Another awkward shrug. 'Not yet. But at least I don't have enemies. That's something, right?'

'Right,' said Hare gruffly.

Now she'd embarrassed him. And exposed herself. Not a place of comfort. Definitely time to flee. 'You ready to send that gondola downhill yet?'

'Just waiting on another passenger.'

'Who?' The ski field had been closed since lunchtime on account of the unpredictable weather. Jolie figured that all the other employees and skiers on the mountain would have headed downhill hours ago. All except for Hare, who lived on the mountain in a cabin half a kilometre away from the main complex.

'Cole.'

'Cole who?' But Hare wasn't answering. Nor was he looking her in the eye. Jolie's stomach began to churn and churn hard. 'Cole *Rees* is here on the mountain?'

'Came up a couple of hours ago. He's up at the lookout.'

'Doing *what*?'

Hare shrugged.

'But...how can he be *here*?' She'd planned her foray to the cabin for a time no member of the Rees family would be anywhere *near* here. 'Why isn't he at his father's funeral?'

'Didn't ask. The man wasn't looking for conversation, Jolie. He was looking for space.'

And now he'd be *sharing* space with her all the way back down the mountain. Just Cole Rees and Jolie Tanner and a box full of evidence of her mother's twelve-year affair with his father. 'Great,' she muttered. 'That's just great. Any chance of rolling another gondola around so that Cole can ride down on his own?' The ski lift consisted of several eight-berth sky gondolas and was a twelve-minute ride, top to bottom.

'None,' said Hare. 'Blizzard warning just came in. You're lucky I'm prepared to run this one.' He looked out of the triple-glazed window of the control hut and nodded once. 'Time to go, girlie. There's Cole.'

Jolie followed Hare's gaze. And there he was. Cole Rees, large as life. Striding down the lookout path towards the gondola, his raven hair windblown and his pretty face set against the worsening weather. A man so reckless, unpredictable and downright *sexy* he made Jolie's insides clench. And that was *before* she factored in his hatred of all things Tanner. 'Great,' she said grimly. 'That's just great.'

Jolie grabbed a ratty sheepskin hat with earflaps from the assortment of old lost-and-found attire hanging on the back wall of the tower and jammed it on top of her beanie. The hat wouldn't be missed, and, besides, she'd give it back. She added a thick black scarf and lost-and-found ski goggles to the ensemble while Hare looked on, deadpan.

'I take it you're keeping my coat,' he said.

'I'll give it back tomorrow.' Not for the first time

today, Jolie gave thanks that she'd worn her oldest ski gear. Unisex attire purchased years ago during a mercifully brief phase in which she'd attempted to downplay her looks and her femininity. Her ski boots were black, chunky, overworn and all about getting the job done. Nothing feminine about them either.

'Hair,' offered Hare.

'Oh.' She took off the hat and goggles, twisted her auburn tresses round and round and then up beneath the beanie, and then jammed the hat back on her head. Her red hair was a legacy from her mother and truly distinctive. Men were fascinated by it. Hairdressers wanted to bottle it. Jolie had no complaints of it, truth be told, but right now she wanted it hidden. She pulled the hat's earflaps down. 'Better?'

'You look like E.T.'s Alaskan cousin,' said Hare. 'I take it that's the point?'

'Yes,' she said, snapping the goggles down over her eyes.

'Or you could be yourself,' murmured Hare.

'No, I really couldn't. Meet JT. J for Josh. He works for you.'

'Go,' said Hare with a roll of his eyes. And as Jolie leaned in to embrace her old minder and mentor, 'Well, don't *kiss* me!'

'Suit yourself.' Jolie gave him a manly thump on his arm instead. 'We going to see you at the bar tonight?'

'If the weather clears,' said Hare gruffly, glancing at his computer screen and the satellite weather map currently dominating it. 'Which it won't. Tell your mama I'll be down for that drink tomorrow night.'

'Will do.'

'And tell her I'm sorry for her loss and mind you say it right.'

'I'll say it right,' said Jolie, with a catch in her voice on account of Hare's deep understanding of her mother's position. Brazen bar owner Rachel Tanner—the bar reputedly a gift from James Rees—would get little sympathy from anyone on account of James's death. Instead she would grieve for her lover in lonely silence. 'I'll practise beforehand.'

Hare just rolled his eyes again and looked out of the tower window and up at the sky. '*Kia waimarie*, little one.' Good Luck. 'Keep your head down. And close up behind you as you go.'

Hare waited until Jolie was out of the door before rubbing at his aching arm again and letting out a sigh. The girl wasn't wrong to want to avoid Cole Rees on this of all days, but whether she *could* was a different matter altogether. Chances were that at some point during the ride down the mountain Cole Rees would look twice at the youth who rode down with him. Chances were that he'd start adding up the inconsistencies.

Hare employed teenagers on the mountain if they had the experience and steadiness he was looking for, but he didn't take them that small. Ever.

Nor did they come with alabaster skin, a delicate jaw and, if a man could get past those lips—and some couldn't—eyes the colour of snow clouds.

It'd be Jolie's eyes that would give her away. No one had eyes like the Tanner women. Not that colour. Not that...*challenge* that lurked in their depths. A siren's mix of sensual self-awareness shot through with aching vulnerability.

Fact: a man could get lost in such eyes and never surface.

He'd seen it happen.

And witnessed the carnage it had caused.

'Eyes down, girlie,' he whispered. 'You give that boy a chance.'

Cole Rees put his head down and quickened his stride as he headed for the ski gondola. The weather matched his mood: filthy and unpredictable, his emotions a roiling mess of sadness and regret, anger and defiance. He hadn't been able to sit through his father's funeral, not all of it. The glowing accolades had turned his stomach. His mother's genuine grief had fuelled his fury. His sister's anxious pleading for him to *please* not make things worse had only cemented his decision to get the hell out of there before he cursed his feted father to rot in hell for eternity.

There would have been no coming back from that.

His mother the society maven would have crumpled completely.

Hannah, his sister, was stronger than that. Hannah would have made him pay dearly for subjecting the family to yet more scandal

Only the gossip mongers would have been satisfied, but not for long. They never were.

He'd wanted a woman to lose himself in—and there were plenty around—but even that small comfort reeked of his father's legacy. Of thoughtlessness and recklessness and appetites not easily sated. And maybe Cole had outgrown thoughtlessness a few years back, and maybe he did his best to check his recklessness, but on that third count he was as guilty as sin.

When it came to women and sexual relationships he didn't satisfy easily. When it came to the mindless use he would make of a woman's body tonight and how little chance she had of engaging his emotions, well… no woman deserved that. Better for everyone to simply practise what his late, great father had never practised and do without.

His mother had organised a wake for after the funeral, but Cole didn't intend to put in an appearance there, either. He'd come up the mountain instead. To mourn his father in his own way and in his own sweet time.

If at all.

The enclosed ski lift was a new addition to the mountain and one he'd been in favour of. It had replaced a series of ageing four-man chairlifts and doubled Silverlake's profits overnight. The sport of skiing had changed. Braving the elements and putting some effort into getting uphill was no longer part of the on-slope experience. Not any more.

These days it was all about comfort.

He looked up at the gondola control-tower windows and sent his father's ski-field manager a wave. Why Hare hadn't been at the funeral was anyone's guess, but the big Maori always had been a law unto himself.

Loyal to James Rees though. Utterly.

A bundled-up youth stepped out of the tower and headed towards the waiting gondola, slipping into step some distance behind Cole and locking down doors and gates behind them. Cole shrugged the snow off his coat and swiped a hand through his hair once he got beneath the boarding station roof. The gondola door stood open and a duct-taped box sat just inside the door. Cole crossed to the opposite wall of the gondola and leaned back against it, hands in his coat pockets for warmth as he waited for the boy to finish closing up.

Cole wasn't dressed for the ski fields. Beneath his heavyweight woollen overcoat he was dressed for a funeral. The only concession he'd made towards the mountain had been to exchange dress shoes for snow boots.

It hadn't been enough. Not for this weather.

The youth finally reached the gondola and slipped inside, shedding snow as he shut the door behind him. Small for one of Hare's chairlift workers, thought Cole absently. Hare usually employed them bigger. Brains aside, brute force was *always* an asset on the mountain and everyone who'd ever worked a mountain knew it.

Hare's sidekick—hell, he was just a kid—settled in beside the box. Feet body width apart, knees slightly bent, he leaned against the wall and window in much the same way as Cole had done. Snowboarder, if the stance was anything to go by. Hardcore, given the mismatched clothes. No fancy be-labelled outfit, no swagger at all, just a quiet competence that drew the eye and held it. This one would be all about the thrill that came of mastering a peak, and the next one and the one after that. Nothing to prove to anyone but himself.

Cole envied him.

His next few months would be all about proving to bankers and shareholders that he was every bit as good as the old man when it came to managing the family holdings. As if he hadn't been raised from the cradle to just this position—learning the Rees businesses from the ground up at his father's command. No quarter asked for and none at all given.

James Rees had been told he was dying two years ago. He'd been handing Rees management over to Cole ever since. Teaching by example. What to do. What not to do. And how to recover. Making Cole admire him in so many ways. Making Cole *care* about the businesses under his control and the people employed within them.

Always two steps ahead of any game, James Rees. Except when it came to thinking that his high-born wife and his stunningly sensual mistress could coexist peacefully in this town.

When it came to that, James Rees had been a fool.

Cole *knew* what his father had seen in Rachel Tanner—he hadn't been blind as a boy and he wasn't blind now. A simmering sensuality that hit a man hard. Unapologetic awareness of a man's deepest desires. Full knowledge of how to satisfy those desires—a knowledge that Cole's puritan, well-mannered mother had wholly lacked.

James Rees had wanted. James Rees had taken. He might have even got away with it if he'd left it at that. If he'd only done it once. Or twice.

Instead he'd had to have it all and to hell with the pain it had caused those around him.

The gondola moved off smoothly while still within the protection of the station walls and roof. And then the wind hit, and snow peppered the windows, and the ride got considerably rougher. It was an automatic response for both Cole and the kid to look up at the cable join, just checking, as the wind lashed against fibreglass walls.

The kid glanced at the intercom on the wall of the cable car next, as if assessing the need to contact Hare. Cole glanced at it too.

'The front's still a way off, according to the forecast,' said the boy finally, his voice cracked and barely audible beneath his scarf.

Cole nodded. He'd seen the storm rolling in from the lookout. The kid would have been monitoring radar loops on Hare's computer deck. Cole adjusted the boy's probable age upwards a couple of years on account of his composure and conversation. No point trying to judge the boy's age from his face—about the only thing visible was his mouth.

Lord, what a mouth.

Cole looked away. Fast.

What the hell was *wrong* with him?

Another gust of wind shook the gondola, slinging it sideways, causing both him and the youth to look up again, always up, to what held them.

Again, the boy glanced at the intercom.

Again Cole studied what he could see of the boy's face beneath the hat and the goggles and the scarf. And looked away, disquieted.

The wind settled, the gondola steadied, nothing to worry about there. Nothing to worry about when it came to his reaction to Hare's chairlift operator, either. Today he was just…off. For too many reasons to count.

Only eleven more minutes of this ride to go.

No point staring out of the window at the view; visibility was down to zero.

Nor did it seem advisable to stare at Hare's lift operator.

That left the box.

Grey-brown in colour, with a removalist's name stamped on the side. Wet at the bottom with one corner slightly concertinaed in. The top of the box patchy damp too, and hastily taped shut. All function over form, just like the youth standing next to it.

The kid shifted restlessly. Cole beat back the urge to look at him and kept his gaze pinned to the box. Just a wet and battered box. Nothing noble about it at all.

Ten minutes to go.

The gondola began to rise as it neared the first of seven cable tower connections. The hair at the nape of Cole's neck started rising too. Hare's youth was studying *him* now; he could damn well feel it.

And his reaction was pure heat.

The lift shuddered, jerked and stopped.

Cole's heart thumped hard and settled to an uneasy rhythm. Probably Hare just slowing them down on account of the wind and the approaching tower. But the gondola did not start inching slowly forwards. It stayed right where it was, swinging hard.

Keeping his hand lightly on the handrail, Cole made his way to the two-way and pulled it from its bracing. Just like the kid, he'd worked the lifts on this mountain and plenty else besides. He knew the drills. 'Hare, you there?'

But Hare did not reply, and neither did the operator supposedly manning the base station. Not good. The kid said nothing, just watched him through those blasted ski goggles and chewed on his full lower lip. Cole's own lips tightened in reply.

'Hare,' he barked. 'Can you hear me?' And when there was still no reply he shoved the two-way back on the wall and fished his mobile phone from his coat pocket. No signal. Not that he'd held out much hope for one. White-out did that.

Damn.

The kid dug a mobile phone from amongst his layers too, and started pressing buttons with a gloved hand. 'No signal here, either,' he murmured.

'I'll call Hare again in a minute,' muttered Cole.

They gave him ten. Ten minutes of uneasy silence, punctuated by a fascination with this boy that Cole didn't even want to try to define.

'Someone should have contacted us by now,' said the youth finally.

What the kid didn't say was that not following procedure meant that in all likelihood Hare had problems of his own up there, and heaven only knew what was happening down below. Base station should have been manned or the gondola should not have been running. Standard Operating Procedure.

'The two-way's not dead,' he said. 'I'll try some other channels. Might raise someone.' Anyone would do.

But there was nothing on the other channels except for static.

Another five minutes passed. Another gust of wind slammed into the gondola, stronger now than it had been. The kid's hands went to the handrail and stayed there as he looked up, always up, to the cable that held them up, his scarf falling away from his face to reveal flawless ivory skin and a jaw that had sure as hell never seen a razor.

Ivory skin? On a ski-lift operator?

'How *old* are you?' The words were out of Cole's mouth before he could call them back. 'Fourteen?' The kid hadn't even reached puberty. 'Fifteen?'

'Older,' said the boy.

'How *much* older?'

'Considerably.'

Considerably? What the hell kind of answer was that?

'Nineteen,' said the kid quickly, as if he had a main-line through to Cole's brain.

'Really,' countered Cole, and the coat shrugged. Cole was beginning to think there was far more coat and hat and scarf than there was kid. *Nineteen, my arse.*

He ran his gaze over the youth again as if looking for…what exactly? Answers? A reason for his fascination? Because he didn't swing that way. Never had before. Didn't think much of starting now.

More minutes passed in uneasy fashion. Not silence— the battering of the wind and the straining of cable fixtures saw to that. But there was no more conversation. And the radio to the outside world stayed ominously silent.

Finally Cole glanced at his watch. Then he glanced at the youth. The boy was still all bundled up, which Cole could fully understand given the plummeting temperature, but what was with the ski goggles staying on? It wasn't as if the kid was going to be getting out of the gondola any time soon.

'You live in town?' asked Cole.

The youth nodded.

'You live alone?' *Not* a pick-up line, may the devil come for his soul if he lied. He needed to clarify his question, clarify it *now*. 'Anyone likely to notice you're missing and raise the alarm?'

'I wouldn't count on it. My—' The boy hesitated. 'My roommate's out of town this afternoon and she'll be working tonight. I come and go as I please.'

Cole sighed and jammed his hands in his coat pockets. So much for the boy's mommy waiting dinner on him and getting anxious when he didn't show. Maybe the kid *was* nineteen. Nineteen, small grown, shacked up with a pint-sized waitress, and perfectly happy with his lot.

Good for him.

'What about you?' asked the youth. 'Is there anywhere you have to be?'

'Yes.'

'So...you'll be missed?'

'I doubt it,' he muttered. And if his mother and sister did miss him, the next thought that ran through their minds would probably be relief. 'I wouldn't count on anyone being alarmed by my absence, put it that way.'

More silence, broken only by the patter of wind driven snowflakes against the shell of the gondola. 'At least we have shelter,' he said. Pity it was fifty metres *up* and hanging from a cable, a very *strong* cable, mind. In a blizzard. 'What's in the box?' he said finally.

'What?' said the kid, looking startled and scared along with it. So much for idle conversation.

'The box,' he repeated gruffly. 'What's in it? Anything we can use?'

'Like what?' said the boy, and his voice was back to being muffled and scratchy and his face was back to being hidden almost entirely by goggles, hat and scarf.

'Like food and blankets,' said Cole. 'If God was good there would also be Scotch.' Although given how muddled Cole's thinking had grown since he'd stepped into this gondola, the lack of fortified beverage probably wasn't such a bad thing.

'There's no Scotch,' muttered the youth. 'It's just some stuff of mine. Mostly junk. I'm finishing up on the mountain today.'

'Mid-season?'

The kid nodded.

'Were you fired?'

'No.'

'Got a better offer?'

'Yes.'

'Somewhere around here?' It was part of Cole's job now, to oversee the running of the ski field. It was the only part of the business empire that James had kept tight control over, the only business operation Cole wasn't wholly up to speed on. If there were staffing problems on the mountain, or if they were losing experienced workers to neighbouring ski fields, Cole wanted to know about it.

'Christchurch,' said the kid.

No ski fields in Christchurch. 'What doing?'

'Not this,' said the kid.

So much for the boy being a dedicated snowboarder, following the snow from season to season in search of the perfect run.

Conversation stopped again. The kid eventually sat on the box and pulled his phone from his pocket. Judging by the tightening of the boy's lips there was still no signal to be had and nothing to do but sit and wait. Or stand and sigh.

'Are you sure there's nothing in the box we could use?' asked Cole eventually. He wasn't usually one to harp but they'd been stuck here for over an hour now, he wasn't getting any warmer, and he was definitely looking for a distraction. 'Even junk has its uses.'

'Not this junk,' said the kid. 'Trust me, there's nothing in this box you want to see.'

'Is that statement supposed to make me want to know

what's in the box *less*?' asked Cole. 'Because—trust me—it doesn't.'

The kid shrugged and declined to answer. Cole studied the boy anew and wondered about the box and what might be in it that would make the kid reluctant to open it in Cole's presence.

'Look, kid. Suppose something *has* found its way into that box that shouldn't be there. A chocolate bar or fifty. A computer no one's using. Ski gear that doesn't belong to you. Do you really think I'm going to give a damn, under the circumstances?'

'Do you really think you won't?' countered the boy. 'Given that it'd be your family I was stealing from? Anyway—' the boy's phone went back in his pocket '—there's nothing stolen in the box. It's just junk.'

'If it's just junk,' murmured Cole silkily, 'why are you protecting it?' And when the kid seemed disinclined to reply, 'So...you know who I am.'

The kid, teenager, young man, philosopher thief, whatever the hell he was, nodded.

'Should I know who you are?'

'No.'

'Because you seem familiar.'

'I'm not.'

'Grew up in Queenstown, though, didn't you?' The kid wouldn't even look him in the eye and for some reason that bit. Was it asking too much to want to get a good look at another person's eyes?

'You don't know me,' the kid said doggedly. 'You don't *need* to know me.'

'Seeing as we're stuck here, I disagree.' *Not* a pick-up line, emphatically not. He just wanted to get a handle on what the kid was trying to hide. 'Didn't anyone teach

you to observe the niceties? Show you how to introduce
yourself?'

'No.'

'Time you learned.' It wasn't as if a handshake would
be required. No touching at all. 'I'm Cole Rees. Cole to
most. Rees, if you prefer. I'll answer to either. Now it's
your turn.'

'Josh,' offered the youth with extreme reluctance.

'It's customary to provide a surname.'

'Not where I come from.'

'Fair enough.' He'd won one concession from young
Josh. Time to make the boy relax before hitting him
up for more. It wasn't as if he couldn't pull the youth's
employment record easily enough once they got out of
the gondola. Right now, though, he wanted something
other than information. He wanted to see the kid's eyes.
'You ever going to take those goggles off, Josh?'

'Wasn't planning to,' said the youth with a curve to
his lips that made Cole suck in a hard breath. The kid's
chin came up. The goggles stayed on. The boy's stance
changed subtly, drawing the eye and confusing Cole's
senses.

'Rees, if you want me to undress, just say so,' murmured the boy. 'Although if we're observing the niceties,
you might want to buy me a drink first.'

CHAPTER TWO

SHE shouldn't have said that. Fifty feet up and with no way of escape, Jolie had just challenged the sexual orientation of a man who'd been loving—and leaving—women since his teens.

Word had it Cole Rees knew exactly how to please a woman. Word had it that he could play all night when the mood took him. *Keeping* Cole Rees's interest for more than one night, on the other hand, had thus far proven impossible. For a woman.

No rumour had *ever* come to her ears about Cole preferring men, but the way the air seemed to have sucked out of the gondola since her rash words... The way his eyes had flashed and his gaze had rested on her mouth before he'd swiftly looked away...

Which would be worse?

Cole Rees's fury?

Or his acquiescence?

And then Cole looked back at her and something in those sharp green eyes of his made her feel as if the ground were falling away from her feet.

Jolie glanced down, adjusted her perch on the box and planted her feet far more firmly on the floor. And waited for his reply.

'Sorry, kid,' he said gruffly, as if he'd been chewing on nails and couldn't quite swallow them. 'You're not my type.'

Silence rained down on them then, heavy and smothering.

'Try the two-way again,' she offered by way of an out, and he did but no one responded.

Cole fell silent again and the silence stretched into eternity. He shoved his hands deep in his coat pockets and stared at his shoes, which left Jolie free to study his face. Not an imperfect line on it. Everything right where masculine beauty demanded it be, with a mouth that spoke of sensuality framed by laughter.

No laughter in him now, but at least he'd stopped hassling her about the box, and he certainly hadn't asked her to take her ski mask off again, only now she was starting to think that there *were* things in the box that they could use. Mittens for starters. They'd probably be miles too small for him, but there were waterproof mitten covers in the box too, and those ones would fit. Herbal teas her mother liked were in that box, along with any other food that might have made a person wonder what it was James Rees had *done* up in his little mountain cabin. The almond biscotti. Godiva soft centres. The bbq salted corn kernels that had come from the bar.

Incidental things like Rachel's shampoo and conditioner. Moisturising cream smelling of jasmine and sandalwood, citrus and rose. Hairbrush and toothbrush. Not a man's things.

Not so incidental things like a digital photo frame full of Rachel's photography.

And then there was the bedspread.

'It's a thousand kinds of black and blue, it's textured

like a Van Gogh, and it's soft,' Rachel had told her with a smile that had broken Jolie's heart. 'It's like sinking into a piece of midnight sky.'

Where it had come from Jolie didn't ask and Rachel didn't say. It was enough that Rachel had wanted to collect it and worried about the when.

Not stolen, Jolie would stake her soul on it.

Given.

A gift for Rachel from her lover.

Quite possibly the only gift Rachel Tanner had ever accepted, for she was no whore, no matter what people thought.

She'd just been painted as one.

The next twenty minutes felt like hours. The weather got worse, more snow—a lot more—and the wind, it just kept coming. Time to get off this ride, past time, but right now that didn't seem likely. If Hare had mechanical trouble up there on the mountain, chances were that the gondola wouldn't move until tomorrow at the earliest—and that was assuming mechanics could even *get* up the mountain tomorrow morning given the amount of fresh snow on the ground. Not that snow wasn't welcome on the ski fields, but this much snow in such a short time boded ill for all.

As for rescue—that'd have to wait until the weather cleared too. The gondola was enclosed—they were out of the worst of it. Crashing to the ground didn't seem likely, in spite of all the swinging. No, the danger most likely to creep up on them throughout the wait would be the cold.

Jolie felt fine. Jolie had more layers on than she needed at this particular point in time.

Cole Rees, on the other hand, didn't.

Scowling, she scooted off the box and ripped off the tape. The gloves were near the top, the bedspread was at the bottom and protected by plastic. Maybe they'd need it eventually. Jolie wasn't quite ready to admit that they needed it now. 'Here,' she said when she'd found the mitten inners. 'Try them.' She held them out.

He studied the mitts, studied her with his fathomless green gaze. 'Got anything in men's?'

'No, but the waterproof covers are in here somewhere.' She dug around for the covers, held them out too. 'They might stretch.'

He took both. He did not let their fingers meet. The inners *were* far too small for him but he tugged them half on anyway. The man was either already beyond cold or pure survival sense had him looking to use whatever he could get when it came to keeping warm. The outers were a better fit. Jolie nodded her approval.

Cole smiled grimly. 'What else you got?'

'Biscuits.' She held up the packet. 'Chocolate.' Up went Lady Godiva. Cole's eyes narrowed. 'Going away present,' she said, improvising fast. 'I think they're out of date, though.'

'Good to know.' Probably just her imagination, the whisper of steel in that deliciously deep voice. 'I do hope there's Scotch. It might be out of date too.'

'There's no Scotch.' She'd left it in the cabin, manly drink that it was. There *was,* however, champagne. Nice little two-hundred-dollar bottle of Dom. She put the biscuits down and held it up. Truly grim now, that beautiful face of his. No point offering any kind of excuse for why it had found its way into the box. Jolie knew full well when to move on fast. Down with the champagne and back out with the biscuits. She opened them, took a couple, and handed Cole Rees the rest. He took them without comment. Ate a handful of them without comment too, while she tried not to watch the way his mouth worked, and his face worked, and how his hair looked as if he'd just rolled out of someone's bed…

Thinking about what Cole Rees might be capable of *doing* to someone in that bed was a very bad idea. Time to look away and tuck her arms around herself and pray they started moving again soon. *Now* would be good.

'More?' His voice was gruff. Jolie jumped and sent him a guarded glance. He was holding the biscuits out.

'No, thanks.'

'When did you last eat?' he asked.

'Lunchtime. When did *you* last eat?' He'd gone through the biscuits fairly fast.

'Yesterday.'

Great, a hungry, angry Cole Rees. 'Eat,' she said, and he snagged a couple more and then twisted the bag shut and came over to the other side of the box and dropped them back in it. He looked. Saw the bathroom products and the teas and the bits and pieces and he made no comment while all around them the wind howled and the gondola swayed and the cable groaned as if it were failing. 'Are you cold?' she asked.

'A bit.' He wiped the condensation from the window with his coat sleeve and looked out. 'Are you?'

'No.' Probably because she had two of everything on. She could give him one of her hats—and might have to. But not yet. She dropped down to a sitting position on the floor, knees up and wide as befitting a boy, and checked her phone again, not for a signal but for the time. Five-eighteen.

Not dark. Not yet.

And then a muffled crack rent the air, the kind of sound no one on a mountainside ever wanted to hear. The kind that reverberated in people's bones and set the world to quaking. 'What was that?' she asked raggedly, scrambling back to her feet with no dignity at all and wiping down her own bit of pane. 'Can you see it?' *It* being an avalanche of the dry-slab persuasion.

'Not yet,' he said, and moved to the top side of the gondola to look upslope.

'Maybe it was just a tree split—'

And then the mountain groaned again and the gondola swung wildly and the box tipped over and tea scattered and the bottle of champagne rolled.

Cole cursed flatly as Jolie scrambled for the bottle and jammed it back in the box and worked the flaps shut. And then Cole grabbed her upper arm and hauled her up next to him to watch as a giant slab of mountain to their right began to move. 'We're not in its path,' he murmured. 'Look.'

He was right, they weren't. But the fear just wouldn't go away. Jolie closed her eyes and clung to the side rail that flanked the gondola door. She could sense Cole behind her, not touching, not quite. She wanted to step back and burrow in deep and cling to him, and not because she wanted to mess with his mind or jump his bones. She just wanted the contact.

'Look,' he said again, his voice a hushed and reverent murmur.

'No, thank you.'

'You'll never see this again. Not from this angle.'

'That better be a promise,' she countered raggedly. But the gondola had steadied so Jolie looked, and caught her breath at the terrible beauty of the earth sliding below them, gathering momentum, cracking, churning.

Foaming.

Shaken, she looked back at Rees, and the fool man went and grinned at her, a crooked, beckoning thing that she didn't want a piece of. Ever.

Time to go, only where *could* they go after *that*? The maintenance teams would be checking the mountain for *days*. Checking the gondola towers and the chairlift fixings and everything else, and that was only the *first* slide. What if there were more?

Jolie didn't care now that she had to brush past Rees to get back to the box and the bottle of champagne. She slid to her knees and started in on the cork, all her considerable years of bar duty coming into play as she popped it, let it foam, and then set the champagne to her mouth.

'Well, that's one way of drinking it,' said Rees dryly, before squatting down beside her and wrapping his big hand around the bottle the better to coax it away from her lips, which he did with ruthless efficiency. 'There *are* others.'

'This way works fine.' At least, it had until he took the bottle away. 'Do you mind?' She gestured for the bottle. 'You're interrupting my panic.'

'I know.' And from the look in those stunning green eyes of his he was going to keep on interrupting it. He took his own pull from the bottle and Jolie watched mesmerised as his throat muscles went to work. He didn't drink much, but by the time he was done Jolie was parched. 'Alcohol and hypothermia don't mix,' he said with more gentleness than she would have given him credit for.

'I'm not hypothermic,' she muttered. 'Yet. I'm in shock. Alcohol is good for shock.'

'So it is.' He held out the bottle for Jolie to take. 'You argue like a girl. You also drink like a girl.'

Jolie stilled, caught between taking the bottle from him and confirming his suspicions, or not taking the bottle from him and confirming his suspicions. In the end she took the bottle and drank, and to hell with her disguise and his suspicions. Her priorities had changed. The prospect of imminent death did that.

'Look, I'm not saying this is an ideal situation but we're safe enough for now,' he said soothingly, leaning in to take the bottle away from her again. 'We have shelter. Food.' He gestured with the bottle and flashed that devil's smile at her again. 'Champagne. And phones that'll work just as soon as this blizzard passes. We're not far from top station. They'll come at us from there.'

Maybe they would. And maybe she and Cole Rees could hold out till then if they stayed calm and thought smart and shared body warmth and all those other things people were supposed to do when stranded in the cold.

'Hey,' he said gently.

Her goggles were fogging up, or maybe it was tears.

'Girl,' he said more gently still. 'Because you *are* a girl, that much I *have* managed to figure out. Take it easy. Lose the panic. It's going to be all right.'

Jolie appreciated the words, she really did.

And then the mountain moved again and this time the gondola moved to meet it.

Down, down, as if in slow motion, still connected to

the cable. That coupling hadn't failed them. Something else had.

Jolie's body didn't want to do what the gondola was doing. Her body wanted to stay up. Cole's body wanted to stay up too. He moved forwards and his arms came around her, pressing her back against the floor, which wasn't the floor any more as the ground rushed up to meet them, nothing slow about the ride now. They were probably going to start another avalanche, if they weren't already riding one.

'Hold on,' he muttered and she did, wrapping her arms around him tight and setting her cheek to his chest. He smelled right. Even through the fear he smelled good.

Small consolation that when it came to his declaration that they were in no imminent danger he'd been dead wrong and she'd been right to panic.

Then the mountain smashed into them and the world went black and being right was no consolation at all.

Jolie woke to discomfort and pain, returning to consciousness slowly, remembering in snatches all that had gone before. The gondola ride. The avalanche. Cole Rees. Laid out on the ground beneath her, out cold but still breathing, and around them a shattered gondola shell half buried in loose snow.

Loose snow. Not avalanche snow, which would have packed in around them like concrete.

The man below her was definitely breathing and she eased off him gently both for her sake and his. Her arms worked and so did her legs, what she could feel of them. Cold, so cold, and Cole was worse. Hatless, nothing waterproof about his coat, his face almost white except for the blood that oozed sluggishly from a cut on his forehead and stained the snow beneath him. Even the blood looked cold and she shed her glove and touched his face…and found it icy to the touch.

Sluggish work to get her goggles off and then the sheepskin hat off her head and onto his, brushing away snow as she went. She put her goggles back on and set her palms to his cheeks, praying warmth reached him in time. 'Cole, wake up.' He stirred and he opened glazed eyes but he'd have to do better than that. 'Cole, *look* at me.'

He tried, bless him, he tried.

'Rees, concentrate.'

'Told you we'd be okay,' he mumbled and started to slip back into the dark.

'No. Cole. Hey. *Rees*. Wake up. Time to go.'

'Good,' he said. 'Go.' He put his hand to his head, which had to be aching. She approved of the movement but she stopped him before he could dislodge the hat and find the blood. 'I'll stay here.'

'No, you'll die here. Cole, concentrate. And *move*. We've lost our shelter. It's almost dark. We need to go.'

'Go where?'

Good question. Not a question she had a ready answer for. 'I think…okay, I think we have two choices. We either stay here and tuck into what's left of the gondola, or… If you think you can climb we try and find our way back to top station. The cable's still attached to something up there. Look.'

He followed her gaze to where the gondola cable did indeed stretch tautly upwards.

'I don't think we should stay here,' she said anxiously. 'Not if you can move. What do you want to do?'

'Climb,' he said after a lengthy pause, and she helped him sit up, and then stand up, and that was how it began, one foot after the other with the cable as their guide.

Jolie fell in behind Rees, and she held her breath every time he went down until he got up again, for she'd never be able to carry him on her own. No, if Cole Rees was to reach the top he'd have to do it under his own steam, which meant tapping into reserves of determination and strength. Or anger and rage. Whatever worked.

'You know what I hate,' she said finally, tapping into her own rage when it looked one time as if Cole wasn't going to get back up. 'People who have everything handed to them on a plate and who then just *give up* at the tiniest little obstacle.'

'That so?'

'Yep.' The accompanying hand she offered him got him mad, but it got him up. 'You know what else I hate?' she said. 'Men who think they can have it all. If I ran hell there'd be a pit especially for them and I'd lower them into it inch by inch until they came to realise that even if they *could* have it all, maybe they shouldn't.'

'You've got a lot of hate in you. You know that, don't you?'

'Tell me about it. I also hate mean drunks and sleazy tippers, but who doesn't?'

'I hate needy conniving women.'

'Me too,' she said emphatically. And as an afterthought, 'You really should try men.'

'So should you,' he murmured. 'Is there any particular reason you're dressed like a boy? You looking to be one?'

'Nope,' she said.

'So…what? You have half a dozen older brothers and you borrow their clothes to go work on the mountain?'

'Nope.'

'So why the disguise?'

'Habit.' That and necessity. And that was that for conversation for a while as they concentrated on getting another fifty metres up that bloody mountain. Halfway to nowhere, with the snow still falling and the wind whipping at their clothes. Jolie was warm enough. Chances were Cole Rees wasn't.

The cable rose above their heads now, good news if it meant they were nearing top station. Bad news in that it gave Cole no stable support. He fell again, and this time he left a dark stain in the snow where his head landed.

'Cole.' She scrambled to her knees beside him. His face was pale, his lips almost blue, and this time his eyes were closed. 'Cole, wake up. C'mon, we're almost there. Talk to me. Tell me what you hate.'

'I saw them together once.' His eyes were still closed. 'Buying clothes.'

'Who?' She grabbed his arm and hauled him upright, tried to get her shoulder beneath his arm to help him up. 'Who did you see?'

'Rachel and Jolie Tanner. And my father.'

'No, you didn't,' said Jolie grimly. She should know. 'Maybe he was just passing by.' She got him to his feet and let him lean on her while he adjusted to being upright and his blood dripped down her cheek.

'Have you seen them?' he said next. 'Rachel Tanner and her daughter?'

'Yeah, I've seen them.' Why was he harping on this? Had he guessed her identity?

'Then you know,' he said.

'Know what?' Jolie slipped out from beneath his shoulder, waited until he'd steadied, and then took the lead, forging a path through knee-deep snow, trying to make it easier going. For him. 'That they're whores?'

'That they're stunning.'

Not what she'd been expecting to hear from this man, though she'd heard it all her life. She glanced back at him but his eyes were on the terrain at his feet. How much longer could he keep going? 'That's hardly a crime.'

'There's this arrogance about them.'

'Bull,' she whispered beneath her breath.

'As if they know what you're thinking and don't give a damn.'

'Maybe it's a defence mechanism.'

'It's maddening, is what it is.'

She didn't dignify his comment with a reply.

'Rachel Tanner kept my father in thrall for over twelve years. She knew he had a wife and children. Responsibilities. She didn't care.'

'Shouldn't *he* have been the one caring about all that?'

'He did care,' said Cole roughly.

'Yeah,' she muttered. 'Just not quite enough to stop his adultery. Paragon that he was.'

'That's my father you're talking about.'

'So it is.' Jolie clamped her mouth shut and let her anger take her further up the slope. Anger was useful.

But it left too fast, ripped out by the wind and the cold, and in its place stood a wall of snow and the first faint stirrings of defeat. 'It can't be much farther. It just can't,' she murmured.

But it was.

They kept moving, with the gondola cable as their guide.

Jolie kept the lead until she'd exhausted herself, and then Cole drew level with her and shot her a glance.

'And then there's the daughter,' he said hoarsely as he trudged past her to take point.

'What *about* the daughter?' Perhaps if he fell over again she could *kick* him up the slope.

'She's exquisite,' he muttered. 'And cunning. She had my father wrapped around her little finger. He got her job after job.'

'He *what*?'

'She never kept any of them.'

'Maybe she didn't *like* any of them,' said Jolie through gritted teeth. *What* jobs had James Rees got her? Dishwasher at the Holiday Inn? Or the Thursday night/Saturday morning slots at the comic-book store? The front-desk job at the tattoo parlour had definitely been her own achievement—that much she did know. All of them had been temporary because they'd had to fit in around her coursework. That was what students *did* when working their way through university hand to mouth.

'Apparently she fancies herself as an artist.'

'Maybe she *is* an artist.'

'It gets better. He bought her a house in Christ-church.'

'He *what*?'

'*Now* do you believe me?'

As a matter of fact she did not. Jolie glared at Cole's broad back and his fancy coat and his stupid, ill-fitting hat. She didn't care that he was hurt and grieving and soaked to the bone. He was wrong.

Jolie stood still, breathing hard, and stared past the idiot in the hat. Past his lies and his hatred as she tried to make out the shape of the slope ahead. Getting to safety was her focus for now. Getting even would have to wait. The cable still ran true and taut, still running upslope towards top station. Was that...?

'Cole,' she said, and when he didn't turn round. 'Cole, look up.'

But he hadn't heard her. She scrambled up beside him and caught at his arm with one hand and pointed with the other. 'Look! It's the station roof.'

He wrenched himself away from her touch and with that motion came the memory of the last time Jolie had touched him, and talked to him. God, it had been *years*.

She remembered the moment as if it had been yesterday.

'Don't touch me,' he said hoarsely.

He'd said the same thing back then too. He'd made her feel like dirt and she hadn't known why. Not then. Not until she'd got home from school that afternoon and Rachel had sat a distraught Jolie down and tried to explain to a twelve-year-old that she'd fallen in love with another woman's husband had Jolie known *why* Cole had recoiled from her touch.

Still recoiled from her touch.

'It's the station roof,' she said wearily, and pointed

towards it, no touching, none at all, and no fight left in
her either.

Cole stopped. He looked up to where she pointed,
his eyelashes white with frost and his eyes muddy with
pain. Maybe he could see the shape of the roof through
the snow, maybe he couldn't. He'd just have to take her
word for it.

'Left or right?' she said next, for they couldn't climb
straight up because of the steepness of the slope and
probably didn't want to anyway. Angling right would
take them to the control tower. Left would get them to
the kiosk for which they didn't have keys. Spare keys
would be in the control tower, which Hare *should* be
manning. Except given the silence of the two-way, Hare
wasn't in right now so chances were the control tower
would be locked up too. 'Cole, left or right? Control
tower or kiosk?'

Jolie didn't know if Cole had the energy for both.

She wasn't sure she did.

'Cole, which way?'

'Kiosk,' he said hoarsely, and they set off again
through the heavy drift. It was up past her knees now
and starting to settle and Jolie prayed for no more ava-
lanches on this steep ground. Hare's boys kept the top
station free of such dangers, as free of them as they
could. Shovelling and raking and occasionally detonat-
ing so that the snow would pack down stable and stay
stable throughout the season.

The transverse across and up to the kiosk took time.
If it wasn't Cole falling, it was Jolie. Their co-ordination
was shot. Cold and fatigue had taken hold.

'Hot chocolate,' she said at one point, when they were

both down, and snow was melting down her neck and her fingers were too numb to get it out.

'Something you hate?' said Cole, struggling upright.

'Something I want,' she muttered. 'And I want it thick and creamy and coating my mouth and I want my hands wrapped around the cup and I'd hold the cup to my cheek and my to lips if I've got any left. I can't even feel my lips any more.'

'Well, they're still moving,' he said, sparing them a glance, and damned if that tiny glance didn't warm her up some.

Cole Rees, nature's antidote to cold.

And then finally, after what felt like hours, they were standing on the kiosk deck and Jolie was clinging to the railing, every muscle trembling, lukewarm tears stinging her eyes. How to get in? She couldn't even *think*.

The door was locked. There were bars on the kiosk windows, mainly to stop skiers skiing into them.

'Restroom window,' said Cole, so they staggered around the side and it was true, there were no bars on that one. But it sat high in the wall and it wasn't very large. Nor was it open.

Again, Jolie stood there, her mind a fog and her body fighting exhaustion as Cole removed his coat and used it and his fist to shatter the glass. 'Up,' he said next, and slid down the wall until he was sitting there with his back against it. 'Use my shoulders. Climb.'

'To do that I'd have to touch you. You don't want me to touch you.' For all her fogginess that part was still crystal clear in her mind.

'It's okay, Red.' His eyes were closed, his lips were blue. 'I can't feel anything any more anyway.'

Jolie climbed him. Fast. Up and in, head first, and then she twisted halfway and got her butt through, hanging onto the window sill with icy fingers as she got one leg in and then the other before dropping heavily to the floor. 'Cole,' she said, but there was no answer. 'Cole, come round to the kitchen door.'

She stumbled through the kiosk kitchen as fast as her half-frozen body would take her. Too much time wasted fumbling with the lock, only to find that Cole wasn't waiting for her when finally she wrenched open the door. Instead, he was right where she left him, slumped beneath the window, barely conscious.

'C'mon, big guy,' she coaxed, and between his efforts and hers she got him to his feet. 'Where's all that legendary stamina?'

He swore at her then, but her goading got them inside. She didn't bother dragging him any farther than the kitchen, just stood him against the wall and told him to stay there as she ripped off her beanie and goggles and turned the gas burners on, as many as she could find, before lunging towards him and planting her shoulder in the middle of his chest to hold him up as he threatened to topple over. The jacket of his fancy suit was soaked through, and so was the shirt beneath it, all the way down to cold, cold skin.

'Gear off,' she ordered, and he tried; his hands came up only to drop back uselessly to his sides. His eyes were closed, his head resting against the wall.

'Buy me a drink first,' he whispered with the faintest of smiles.

'That'll be the day,' she muttered as she started in on his too-tight mittens, and then his jacket and shirt. The man was all muscle and no fat and at some other time she might have taken the time to admire such a chest but he was far too cold for that, and she was far too worried about him. She shrugged out of Hare's coat, waterproof and warm. She got him into it and buttoned it up and he shuddered hard. 'Better?'

'Better.'

He still had the hat on. She slid cold fingers beneath the hat and into his hair and he trembled again but it was warm in there, warmer than her hands at any rate, so she left it on him.

He had waterproof snow boots on, hopefully they'd saved his feet from frostbite, but his trousers would have to come off and that meant boots off too. She knelt and set to work and he tried to help by shaking them off and succeeded only in planting her on her butt. She got them off him eventually, co-ordination central not, and then with only the slightest hesitation she got to her knees and found his trouser fastening.

He protested at that, tensed up hard, slid his hand through her hair, and forced her head back. 'If this is about modesty—' she began, and then looked up and met his glazed gaze with her own. There was no shock in his eyes, just weary recognition.

'I knew it was you,' he murmured. 'The minute you grabbed my arm like that, I knew it was you.'

'Yeah, well. Enjoy the touch.'

He swore then, a nice colourful little invective that summed up their situation nicely and also reminded her what *not* to do with this man. Ever.

He let go her hair and batted her hands away from his trouser fastenings. He tried to undo them himself without much luck.

'I'd have had them off you by now,' she murmured,

holding his gaze with a challenging one of her own as she stood and sought his fingers with hers and between them they got the clasp undone and the zipper down and all the while his gaze didn't leave her own. Lots for her fingers to avoid brushing over down there; she'd heard that about him too.

'Back off, Red,' he whispered.

Lots.

She backed up fast, hands in the air, hold-up style, her cheeks warm, even if the rest of her wasn't. 'You need to check for frostbite,' she said.

'So do you.'

'My hands are fine. I can feel my toes.' She turned and spread them back over the cooking burners, giving him privacy. 'I'll shed my jeans in a minute. There should be a hypothermia kit on the rack by the back door. Thermal blankets. Fire blankets. Aprons.'

She heard him move. She heard something hit the wall and turned to find Cole right where she'd left him only minus the trousers, shoulder to the wall this time, and sporting a fresh pallor.

'Give me a minute,' he murmured. 'I'm just…' He closed his eyes.

'Oh, no, you don't. C'mon, Rees, eyes open.' She got in front of him, up close and personal, the better to prop him up. 'Think of all the liberties I'd take if you passed out on me now. I'd go on a shopping spree with your fancy platinum credit card the minute the Internet came back online.'

'Buy me some dry trousers,' he said faintly.

'I'll steal your phone and take photos of the new head of the Rees empire getting cosy with the kitchen floor.

I'll send them to everyone in your address book. They'll think you've been drinking.'

'Wouldn't be the first time.'

'I'll have to undress the rest of you. Think of your modesty!'

'Think of it this way, Red,' he murmured. 'At least if I'm unconscious I'll behave.'

And then he passed out.

She crumpled to the floor with him, sparing him bruises and collecting a few more of her own, cursing herself for too much talk and not enough heat being generated. Hard to believe given the sexual tension that had crackled between them just moments before, but unconscious men didn't lie. What the hell did he mean with the crack about behaving? Surely he didn't *like* it when she touched him? Did he?

Jolie eased out from beneath him, gentle with him now, because she'd heard that you should be gentle with hypothermia patients. Careful with his head because, as irritating as Cole Rees was, she badly wanted him to stay alive.

What to do for someone with hypothermia and concussion? Active rewarming or passive, now that there was food and warmth and dry clothes at their disposal? Should she check his head wound or leave it be? She'd done a first-aid course eons ago and remembered about half of it. Never had she had to put any of it into practice.

Jolie gritted her chattering teeth, willed her memory to return and set to work removing his socks. Removal of his boxer shorts came next. Cole Rees wasn't going to be a happy camper when he came to.

If he came to.

'Trust me, I'm hard to impress.' She slid her fingers inside the band of his boxers, and eased them over the bulky bits, deliberately not looking as she slid them over thighs better suited to a slalom skier than a desk jockey. Strong legs. Powerful.

Okay, so maybe she was a little impressed. But she still hadn't looked at all of him, and didn't intend to look, looking being the first step on the slippery slope to wanting, and wanting being *out* when it came to this particular man.

'You know what they're going to do to me if you die?' she muttered as she went for the thermal blankets and the fire blankets and found an old sleeping bag too. 'They're going to lower *me* into that hell-pit feet first. They're going to say we should have stayed with the gondola, and maybe we should have, but we didn't, and that was *your* call just as much as mine, so wake up, Cole. I'll be needing you to take at least some of the blame.'

She made a bed beside him, a mad mix of fire blankets and space blankets and the sleeping bag on top. She got him out of Hare's coat because the outside of the coat was still wet. The man was naked now, and this time she couldn't *help* but look as she rolled him onto the bedding. The man was a masterpiece. Beautiful everywhere. Even cold.

The kiosk's hypothermia kit had heat pads, two of them. She cracked the layer between the chemicals to start the thermal reaction and then wrapped them in tea towels and tucked them beneath Cole's armpits. She tucked the sleeping bag tightly around him and put another thermal blanket on top of that. What next?

'Here's what we're going to do,' she muttered grimly.

'I'm going to clean your head wound. Then you're going to warm up, and wake up, and thank me very nicely for my efforts. No house. No diamonds. A simple thank you will do. And then when we get back to Queenstown and everybody asks you what it was like being stuck on a mountainside with me, you're going to go very quiet and then you're going to say—in front of God, your family, your fancy friends and half the town— "I may not have been entirely comfortable in Jolie's company, but she kept me alive, and she has my thanks." Is that really too much to ask? That for once in your life you and your sister and your mother stop *hating* me for something that was never my fault?'

'Jolie,' he whispered threadily, and she leaned in close the better to hear him. Cole's eyes were still closed and he lay very still, but at least he was conscious again, or something close to it.

'What?' she muttered. 'What *now*?'

'You talk too much.'

CHAPTER THREE

COLE woke slowly, with limited recognition of his surroundings. The bed he lay on was warm but not soft. The woman in his arms had underwear on but he didn't. Not a regular occurrence. He had a splitting headache. Also not a regular occurrence. Alcohol wasn't his vice, and he steered clear of chemical stimulation. Women *were* a weakness of his, and a slow slide of his hand beneath her vest and across her back assured him that this one was indeed exquisitely shaped, but why wasn't she naked? And why didn't his body feel suitably...rested?

Because his body was telling him there was work to be done here, and his mind was telling him something entirely different, namely 'whoa, back' and 'bad idea' and he was on his back and she was tucked tightly into his side, half on top of him with her leg slung over him for good and possessive measure, her slight form no weight at all, and since when had he *ever* slept soundly with a woman in his arms, not to mention on top?

Never, that was when.

His eyes felt gritty and his head... He wished to God his head belonged to someone else. What had he been *doing*?

He remembered his father's funeral clearly enough.

He remembered trying to make sense of his conflicting feelings about the death of a father he'd loved, and his feelings on the death of that same man whose actions Cole had often abhorred. He didn't remember anything of his father's wake. Maybe he *had* gone drinking. Maybe he'd got completely hammered and taken a woman to his bed to console him. Not exactly what a good son would have done, but then Cole wasn't one.

So who was she?

Cole opened his eyes and glanced down and quickly shut them again. A redhead. Not carroty red but truly Titian and glossier than a raven's wing. Cole *never* bedded redheads. They reminded him too much of his father and—

And then he remembered everything. The boy in the gondola. The avalanche, and the gondola coming down. The trek to the kiosk. And her.

Jolie Tanner. *The* Jolie Tanner.

Hated since childhood for the sins of her mother.

Avoided ever since for sins that were all her own.

Wanted…

Cole's body certainly thought so.

Wanted for quite some time now if he was being brutally honest…but only in the sense of a spoiled child wanting the one thing his parents had denied him.

So he'd been attracted to her, so what? Most men were.

He'd never followed through.

And then Jolie moved in her sleep, her lips brushing his shoulder and her body sliding ever closer towards true intimacy and he groaned aloud and brought a hand up through her hair, presumably to persuade her to rearrange her body elsewhere.

Except that his hand stayed right where it was and so did she.

Eyes still closed and cursing himself for ten different kinds of fool, Cole didn't move her anywhere. Her body was soft and pliant and deliciously warm. Not a boy. Emphatically not a boy as she sighed and straddled him more fully. Not awake yet, her body told him that, but he was painfully awake now and all the way aroused, and tortured restraint was new to him.

What now? What now for him and the woman who'd goaded him to the relative safety of the kiosk, dragged him inside, stripped him and chosen to warm him in time-honoured fashion before succumbing to her own exhaustion?

I am not my father.

Cole Rees was *not* in the habit of taking whatever he wanted and to hell with the consequences. He knew better than that.

Wake her up. Get her off him. Find some painkillers and take them. Get his head on right.

And then she moved and made a sound a kitten might make as it burrowed closer for warmth and Cole moved with her, aligning his body so that his hard length nestled against the vee of her panties. He groaned again, because he shouldn't be doing this and he was, and it was so goddamn erotic, and his hands had a mind of their own as they slid down her back. Slowly, so slowly, he traced his fingertips down her spine, savouring the texture and the shape of that which he could not have.

She moved again, a tiny rocking rhythm that rubbed her against him, back…and forth. His fingers had reached the rim of her panties now. Time to stop. Past time to stop.

'Red,' he rumbled, wanting her awake, wanting his mind back. 'Wake up. Get off me.'

Slowly, as if coming out of drugged sleep, Jolie Tanner put her hands to his chest and pushed herself up into a sitting position, her lips parted and her eyes smoky and slumberous as she stared down at him.

Her hair tumbled around a face that would haunt him for ever, and as for the feel of her...

'Red,' he said hoarsely. 'You really need to get off me.'

'I heard you the first time,' she murmured, but she didn't move a muscle and neither did he.

And then she slowly rocked against him again and his hands encouraged her, tightened on her buttocks, guiding her, wanting so much more of her. Her hands palms down on the bedding on either side of his face now and her lips hovering mere inches above his.

'How's your head?' she whispered.

'Bad.'

'I did what I could.'

'I know.' Barely a growl now, his voice, and as for his palms, they rode high on silken thighs and his thumbs were skating beneath the elastic of her panties, wanting in. 'Jolie—' An order. A plea. A last-ditch attempt to summon sanity.

'I know.' Her lips were closer now. 'Get off.'

'Now,' he commanded as his thumb slipped beneath her panties and found her slickness and her centre.

'Okay.' As she caught her luscious lower lip between her teeth and made that tiny rocking movement again.

They were so screwed.

'You don't like me touching you, remember?' she whispered raggedly.

'I remember.'

'You thought I was dirt.'

'That wasn't the reason.' As his thumb moved and his brain grew ever foggier. 'One kiss, and then you *have* to get off me,' he murmured. 'Just one.'

'Just one,' she echoed, and then her lips touched his, soft and tempting. Barely a kiss at all until he risked slanting his head and taking it deeper, ignoring the bellowing of his skull in favour of tracing the lush seam of her lips with his tongue.

He wanted in. Had to taste her just once. Couldn't believe how much he wanted to be buried inside her, just once.

Crazy man thinking. Not for him, Jolie Tanner.

Forbidden.

And then she opened her mouth and he tasted her and fell off the end of the Earth.

Jolie knew it was wrong to want him like this. She should have got off him when he asked her to, only he'd been so warm and his hands, they knew... All the things her body craved, he knew...

He kissed like a man who knew how to savour that which pleased him. His taste went to her head and chased away reason as he pushed her panties to one side and replaced cotton weave with a silken shaft. One kiss that went on for ever as he positioned her, or she positioned him, and he inched his way inside her.

Still the same kiss, though only the bow of their upper lips touched now as she gasped and he cursed and they moved and pleasure soared.

How could he know...? How did he know that running his fingertips slowly down her spine would turn her insides to liquid and allow him such deep possession?

So much sensation and all of it overwhelming as he deepened their kiss again and moved inside her as if caught in a sweet and languid dream. Stunning man with his hard body and slow hands and a way about him that brought her soaring into orgasm long before she ever had before, breaking off their kiss, their one kiss, to testify aloud to the pleasure he'd wrought in her.

Passion made sharp by denial as she buried her face in his neck to muffle her cries only then he groaned too, and his arms banded around her fiercely tight, and his hands came up to cradle her head and press her mouth to his skin. He thrust into her, urgent now, and she rode a second wave of pleasure because of it and bit down hard on skin and lit him up.

Up and into her, over and over, as hot seed spilled deep inside.

CHAPTER FOUR

JOLIE tried to wish herself away in the aftermath of Cole's possession and her surrender. It didn't work. She'd tried to wish herself away in the gondola too—that hadn't worked, either. Maybe she could try wishing them back into the gondola instead, that being infinitely preferable to what had just happened here.

One kiss. Just one. And a lovemaking session so close to perfect it would haunt the rest of her days. Incandescent, deeply sensual, soul-exposing lovemaking.

With Cole Rees.

She didn't look at him as she slid off him, all the way off him, and scrambled from the makeshift bed. His arms had tightened round her when first she began to move but after that he'd let her go, and when she glanced back at him—just once—on her way to the bathroom he was exactly where she'd left him, fresh lines marring his forehead and his eyes closed.

Clean-up time, sordid and shameful, her panties wet with Cole Rees's semen and his scent, her body trembling with cold now, rather than unspeakable pleasure.

What had they done?

More to the point, how could they undo it?

Amnesia would be good. Selective amnesia, along the lines of being able to remember everything *but* Cole Rees's lovemaking. Denial would work too. Just go back out there and find Hare's coat and put it on and pretend nothing out of the ordinary had happened. Not for Jolie Tanner, who clearly did this sort of thing all the time.

What she wouldn't give for a shower so that she could wash away every trace of him, of what they'd just done, but she made do with paper hand towels and warm water from the tap, and when finally she stepped from the bathroom every defence mechanism she'd ever cultivated was primed and ready for use.

Cole Rees meant nothing to her, ergo he couldn't hurt her. Hadn't hurt her. Their liaison was just…unfortunate, that was all. A product of circumstance and forced proximity, and…and…finding themselves *alive* after being so close to death. Oh, yeah, that excuse was a goodie. She could work with that.

Cole Rees was standing by the cooktops when she returned, the sleeping bag zipped up around him and the hood on his head holding it up. A saucepan of milk sat warming on one of the burners.

He sent her a swift, searching glance and she returned it with a measured look of her own. Hard to maintain what he called arrogance and she called defensiveness when wearing damp cotton boy bottoms and a vest top, but if the narrowing of his eyes and the tightening of his lips were any indication she managed it.

Jolie found her ski jacket and slipped it on, grateful for its protection never mind that it was cold to the touch. It covered her from neck to thigh and would soon warm up and so would she.

She spared him another glance. One arm and a

shoulder were out of the sleeping bag now as he jiggled the saucepan, and the hood had slipped around to expose the cord of his neck where she'd grazed him with her teeth. He'd liked that. His control had shattered completely when she'd done that.

'I thought coffee might help,' he said grimly. 'Or hot chocolate or something. You want some?'

Jolie dragged her gaze away from his neck and tried not to flinch as she looked into his fierce green eyes and saw the warning there. *Don't go there,* that look said, and she was more than happy to comply.

Denial it was.

'Yes,' she said and found her boots and shoved her feet into them before heading for the cool room where the kiosk staff kept the food. 'What do you want to eat?' She didn't mind putting something together for both of them, it'd give her something to do. 'I see hams and cheeses and leftover carrot cake.' Leftover Turkish bread too, so she piled them up in her arms and all but bumped into Cole on the way out. He backed off with excruciating politeness and what looked like a screaming need to be far, far away.

Oh, she knew the feeling.

He returned to the stove and busied himself with the making of coffee for himself and hot chocolate for her, while she made sandwiches for toasting and cut two generous wedges of cake.

Sex made her hungry. So did traipsing up mountains in a snowstorm. Nervousness, on the other hand, made her lose her appetite completely.

She figured her appetite for moderate, right up until she bit into the cake and discovered herself ravenous.

'How long do you think it'll be before they get people

up here?' she asked between bites. The clock on the wall said three-fifteen and she figured it for a.m. rather than p.m.

'Maybe a couple of days,' he said. 'Sooner if anyone realises we're missing and were headed this way to begin with. My trip up here wasn't exactly planned.'

'Mine was,' she offered quietly. 'My mother knew I was up here and I might have been missed by now. I'd say chances are fifty-fifty. I was due at the bar last night for a drink.'

'Maybe he figured you for a no-show.' Cole Rees couldn't quite keep the bite out of his voice. 'Easy come, easy go and all that.'

'Only for you,' she murmured, truly hating him in that instance. 'For what it's worth I was going to have a drink with my mother and anyone else who wanted to raise a glass to the memory of the man she'd loved without question for years. Go on,' she said, with as much contempt as she could spare, given that most of it was currently reserved for herself. 'Ask me who he was.'

'You bitch.' Cole Rees had a temper.

'You provoked me.' Jolie eyed him just as hotly. 'We'll get along much better if you don't.'

'Maybe,' he murmured. 'Wouldn't be nearly as interesting, though, would it?'

Interesting wasn't quite the word she'd have used for this encounter. *Horrifying* seemed a hell of a lot closer to the mark, what with the almost dying, and then the life-affirming coitus, and now the childish bickering…

Jolie bit into her cake with more anger than delicacy and tried to ignore him. Hard to do when the cream cheese frosting ended up on her lips and she had to lick it off, and Cole's eyes darkened and he stabbed into *his* cake as if executing a demon or ten.

'One kiss,' she said, throwing him a dark glare. 'That's what you said. *One.*'

'It *was* just one,' he countered grimly.

'And the rest?'

'That was…unwise,' he muttered, his gaze on her mouth again momentarily before he hastily turned away. Maybe she still had cream around her mouth? Hastily she wiped her hand over the lower part of her face. Nope.

Jolie studied Cole's hands as he brought the simmering milk over to the counter and started fixing the drinks. He chose to make instant coffee and hot chocolate, rather than wrestle with the cafe's espresso machine that he might or might not have known how to use. Jolie didn't care how he made her hot chocolate so long as it was hot and sweet and soothing. A little bit of soothing would go a long way towards settling the knives in her stomach every time she looked Cole's way.

So he had nice hands. Big, square-palmed, long-fingered hands. So he used those hands in ways that were slow and sure and put a woman in mind of a song that recommended a lover with an easy touch. Surely the way Cole had savoured the feel of her against him wasn't *that* uncommon? He wasn't the only one out there who knew what it was to honour a woman's body and her needs. There were plenty of men out there who could satisfy her the way he had. *Plenty.*

She just hadn't found them yet.

'Sugar?'

'What?' she said, still lost in the imaginary world of plenty. 'Oh, yes. One sugar. Thank you.'

He handed it over and Jolie sipped her hot chocolate while she found a pan for toasting sandwiches and went back to the cool room for margarine. Cole ate his cake while Jolie fried the sandwiches, the heat of the pan a welcome distraction from the heat of Cole's brooding gaze. They ate the sandwiches in silence, and the knowledge that she was safe and warm and fed and that there was nothing else to do but wait for the blizzard to pass was enough to make Jolie's eyelids droop and her shoulders slump. Her day might have started out with a sleep-in and a lazy brunch, but it had got considerably more demanding thereafter. She couldn't even contemplate the kind of day Cole had put in.

Somewhere amongst it all had been a funeral.

'You should get some sleep,' said Cole Rees coolly. 'You look tired.'

'What about you? What'll you do?'

'I'll stay up for a while. See if I can raise Hare. Or base. Anyone. Let them know where we are and not to go looking for us on the slopes.'

Jolie looked longingly at the bedding piled up on the ground. Her legs were cold and her jeans were still damp and not for putting back on just yet. The makeshift bed was mighty hard but she could snuggle down into it and get warm and dream of fluffy bed socks. Clean, dry socks being her second-best fantasy of the moment, right after the hot-shower fantasy in which she scrubbed Cole Rees from her skin and her memory.

'Go,' he murmured. 'Get warm. Get some rest.'

'But what if you get tired? Or your head gets worse? And don't you look at me as if you're invulnerable because I know damn well how close you came to freezing. I was there.'

Hard for a man wearing nothing but a dove-grey sleeping bag to look haughty but Cole Rees managed it.

Jolie just raised an eyebrow and waited.

'If I need to lie down I'll wake you,' he said finally. 'Then we can either swap places or rearrange the bedding so that we don't—'

'Exactly,' said Jolie hastily. No need to elaborate. 'That'll be fine.'

With one last wary glance for Cole, Jolie headed for the pile of bedding and started burrowing into the layers.

'Just one more thing that needs to be clear between us,' she murmured, her coat still buttoned to her neck as she tried to find the most comfortable spot within the blankets. 'My mother never took money from your father. Or jewellery. Or clothing. Or houses. Or favours. She bought the bar with money that came to us when *her* mother died. My mother came from a wealthy family, you see. Not that anyone around these parts would believe it. Your mother and all her cronies made sure of that.'

Cole Rees glared at her. Jolie glared back. She wasn't finished yet. There was more. Years and years more and she'd lived every minute of them.

'My mother's a very good businesswoman. The bar runs at a decent profit. Your father had *nothing* to do with that. As for me, I work as a graphic artist for a film special effects studio in Christchurch. As far as I know I got the job on my own merit. I live in a one-bedroom rental I can barely afford. I have education debts that I'm still paying off. And I sure as hell don't own any house.'

'Have you finished?' he said, icily polite.

'No. I've lived in the shadow of your father's affair with my mother since I was twelve years old. I never wished James ill…*I did not*…but now that he's gone, I hope to hell the shadow he cast goes too, because I *hated* it. I hated the rifts it created. I hated the way rich boys like you looked at me and wondered how much it was going to cost them to get in my pants. I hated the reputation I got without ever earning it, because it was a reputation that stuck, no matter how I tried to fight it. I hate the way men in this town treat me as if I'm something to be conquered and the women here take one look at me and decide I'm out to enslave their men.'

Cole said nothing.

'So I'm telling you plain, and I'm saying it twice in case you didn't quite catch it the first time round. I received *nothing* from your father, and I sure as hell *want* nothing now that he's gone. Don't presume to know me *or* my mother, because you don't. Don't presume to judge us without looking to the failings of your own family first. If you can manage a little garden-variety courtesy I'd be surprised, but also grateful. Failing that, leaving me alone would work too.'

'*Now* are you finished?' he asked in a soft, lethal voice that set Jolie to swallowing and wishing she hadn't been quite so forthright.

'Yes.'

'Good. Go to sleep, Red. I can't speak for my sister or mother but rest assured that if you and I ever get down off this mountain and run into each other again I shall be civil. I shall be courteous. And I will definitely be leaving you the goddamn hell alone.'

* * *

Jolie slept the rest of the night away. Cole woke her at ten a.m. the following morning with the smell of bacon and eggs and the sound of coffee beans grinding. Apparently he did know how to use the espresso machine. That or he'd figured it out in the hours she'd been asleep. He looked exhausted but his eyes were clear and his gaze was measured as she stirred and sat up and rubbed at her face to chase away the last of the sleep.

'How do you feel?' he said from his post by the cooker.

'Like I crashed into a mountainside, fought my way through a snowstorm, and fell asleep on the floor.' She pushed her hair out of her face and discovered a tenderness of jaw she hadn't noticed last night. Tenderness in other places too. 'I don't suppose anyone clouted me while I slept?'

'Funny girl.' But his eyes were sharp on her face. 'It looks bad.'

'It probably feels better than it looks,' she said, working her fingertips gingerly over her cheek. 'I mark easily. Goes with the colouring. How about you? How's the head?'

'Woolly, though that might be from the painkillers I found in the medical kit. I can't remember half of how we got here. I don't remember getting undressed.'

'Good,' she said, getting to her feet and hunting down her snow boots. 'It wasn't memorable.'

Much.

'I do remember promising you a certain level of courtesy,' he said, and paused long enough for Jolie to mentally list all the events that had occurred in *between* Cole's getting naked and his grimly delivered vow of courtesy. She stopped just short of replaying in her mind their unfortunate slip into the land of mutually intense sexual satisfaction. She still couldn't find a good enough reason for why they'd done that. 'How do you like your bacon and eggs?' he asked next.

'Crispy and sunny side up. Thank you,' she said, common courtesy not being his province alone. 'Did you manage to get anyone on the radio?'

Cole nodded. 'Twenty minutes ago. The crew at base station now know we're here. They're letting your mother know. And mine.'

'Oh,' said Jolie faintly. 'That'll go down well.'

'Indeed,' he murmured as he scooped her egg out onto a nearby plate. He flipped the other eggs in the pan and pushed the bacon about. 'No one's been able to raise Hare. They're sending a helicopter up as soon as there's a gap in the weather, which they're predicting will be within a couple of hours.'

Jolie nodded. Surely they could manage the next hour or two together in civilised fashion? If she kept her mouth shut and her opinions to herself... If Cole did the same, and they avoided all talk of family. 'Hare should have called in by now,' she said quietly.

'I know.'

'Should we look for him? Not mountainside, I know, but we could check the control tower and whether the ski mobile's gone or not. We might even be able to get out to Hare's cabin.'

'No,' said Cole. 'I think we should leave it for the rescue crew to look for Hare. They'll be here soon enough and they'll come prepared.'

'But—'

'Jolie, we don't have the clothes and we don't have specialised equipment. If Hare's been out in that all night he's not going to be in good shape. If he's holed up in one of the buildings he should be fine, just like us.'

'Can we *not* use the *us* word?' So much for keeping her mouth shut. 'I'm really not comfortable with it.'

'I'm guessing you'd rather I didn't use the phrase *together* when talking about us, either,' he said blandly. Jolie shot him a worried glare. Cole favoured her with a dangerously angelic smile. 'As in you and me—meaning we—battled the elements together, struggled to safety together… I think we should get our story straight now, don't you? Because heaven knows people are going to ask you and me what happened. Note how I avoided using the word *us*, by the way. As requested.'

'You are such a gentleman.'

'Occasionally I try.' Cole turned off the heat to the pan, scooped the remaining egg out onto another plate, and divvied up the bacon before adding toast and bringing both plates over to the bench and setting the one with the sunny-side egg in front of her. He found cutlery and put a set in front of her. 'So where were we storywise?'

'We struggled to safety,' she said. 'We could probably stop there.'

'Agreed. It's not as if anyone will want to know if we came together as one in our efforts to stay warm. I've always liked that phrase, by the way. *Coming together as one*… It implies a certain level of…competence, wouldn't you say?'

No, it implied a certain level of needling on his part, about an event she was trying desperately to forget.

'It's not a phrase that appeals to me,' she offered tightly. 'It's trite. Sentimental. It also implies an emotional intimacy that for most people simply isn't there. As for competence—all competence requires is a bit of practice and certain basic skills. You really should be aiming for excellence.'

'That's right, I forgot,' he murmured silkily. 'You like to come first.'

He really shouldn't have put non-plastic cutlery in front of her. What if she decided to stab him with it?

He smiled at her as if he knew her thoughts, and picked up his own cutlery and tucked into his meal.

Eyes narrowed, Jolie did the same. It wasn't to her advantage right now to point out the latest manner in which he liked to come. As in hard and long. Inside her.

'Are you likely to get pregnant?' Cole kept his gaze on his plate and his hands busy with loading up his fork, but his words were clear enough, and they hung there, blade sharp and shiny.

'No,' she said coolly.

'I'm not usually so careless.'

'And you think I am?'

'I didn't say that.' This time Cole's bright green gaze did meet hers, heavy on the frustration. 'Look, just call me if anything comes of this.'

'It won't.'

'How can you be so sure?'

'Cole, I appreciate the belated concern—I really do—but I'm well protected against such an event. Let's just assume for now that *nothing* is going to come of this. That way, when we finally get off this mountain top we can forget all about what happened, and move on with the rest of our very separate lives. You get to be master of all you survey here in Queenstown, I'll go back to my job in Christchurch, and everyone gets to live happily ever after.'

'It won't be as easy as you think,' he muttered. 'Forgetting what happened up here.'

'I didn't say I thought it would be easy. Just necessary.'

'Is it?' he said finally, and something in his sombre gaze made Jolie tense and tremble. 'Maybe I can buy you a drink some time.'

'Cole, don't do this.'

'Why not?'

'You *know* why not. What are you asking for? The same sort of set-up your father had with my mother? The answer's no.'

'That's not what I was asking for,' he said grimly.

'What, then? Your usual? One night? Haven't we done that already?'

Cole's eyes flashed with a warning Jolie chose to ignore.

'Here's a thought,' she murmured, defensive beyond reason at the thought of allowing Cole Rees close enough to hurt her, at the thought of him *wanting* to get close enough to hurt her. 'How about champagne and roses and a loving partner for Jolie Tanner? Someone who's proud of her and supportive of her and doesn't give a damn what other people think or say about her?'

Cole said nothing.

'Yeah, that's what I thought,' she said bleakly. 'I'm sorry, Cole, but you and I…what happened up here in the dark when no one was watching…I can't do that out in the open with you. Even if the feel of you inside me was…intense. I just can't. And neither should you.'

* * *

Cole spent the next two hours pacing. He couldn't settle and didn't want coffee. He still had no phone signal. He didn't want food. What he *wanted* was a woman who didn't challenge his every move. One who would've said yes to that drink and bored him within moments of doing so.

Only Jolie hadn't said yes and she hadn't bored him yet.

Screwed with him, yes. Taunted him, challenged him, blamed James for all manner of things. But she hadn't bored him.

She'd found a copy of yesterday's paper and started filling out the Sudoku. When that was done she started in on the crossword. She had a habit of tapping the top of the pen against her lips. He had a nasty habit of getting aroused every time she did so.

It seemed like an eternity before the radio crackled to life again and the base crew informed them that the helicopter was on its way. In reality only an hour and a half had passed.

'They're on their way?' she asked when he finished the call, even though she had to have heard most of it. He nodded. Time to get out of the sleeping bag and back into his clothes, even if half of them were still damp. Appearances were important and apparently Jolie Tanner thought so too, because she favoured him with a tight smile as she walked past him, collected her jeans from the kitchen chair she'd hung them over, and disappeared into the ladies' room.

Maybe she would be able to make herself look as if she hadn't just tumbled out of his arms and his bed. Maybe between them they could convince people that nothing untoward had happened.

The problem being that something very untoward had happened between them, and, like it or not, he wanted it to happen again. In a proper bed this time and with all the time in the world to explore what could happen when all their antipathy and awareness translated into something else entirely.

He was mad to even consider it.

Not like father, like son.

He at least knew what his actions would cost the people around him. How much it would hurt his mother and Hannah to take up with Jolie Tanner just when they thought they'd finally buried the unwelcome association between Tanners and Reeses. Time now for Cole to forget all about grey-eyed waifs with alabaster skin, and a tongue that could strip the defences from a man's soul.

'You're right, we can't,' he said to the room at large and no one at all. 'Glad we sorted that out.'

Dropping the sleeping bag to his feet and stepping out of it, Cole collected up his clothes and started pulling them on, erection and all.

The helicopter arrived soon after, bringing with it four orange-overall-clad rescue workers and a pilot. Two rescuers headed for the control tower. The other two headed towards Jolie and Cole.

Cole didn't see much point in lingering and Jolie certainly seemed amenable to moving on, so they started out and met them halfway. Knee-deep in drift, amidst smiles and introductions, and then all four of them headed for the chopper.

The rotor blades had stilled, but the pilot still sat at the controls, flicking switches, speaking into his headset. 'How bad is the avalanche site?' Cole asked the older of the two men, the one who'd said his name was Abe.

'The slab missed base station and the ski field car park by half a kilometre. That's your good news,' offered Abe. 'The bad news is that you've lost two gondola towers, three gondola units, chairlifts two and eight are gone, and there's an almighty mess of snow in the valley below yours that's causing some concern on account of it triggering another bigger slide. Snowfall's been heavy enough to cause concern in lots of places but so far, you've been hardest hit.'

'So much for breaking it to him gently,' murmured Jolie and earned herself sharp glances from Abe and co, and a tiny smile from Cole.

'How'd you get the knock on the head?' Abe asked him.

'We were in one of the gondolas when it went down.'

'You were *what*?' Abe looked incredulously at Cole. 'You said you were in the kiosk. The assumption being that you'd waited out the entire blizzard in the kiosk.'

'No.'

'*Now* you tell us.'

'Didn't seem much point telling you earlier. We're fine. Is there anyone else unaccounted for on the mountain?'

'Only Hare,' said Abe.

'He was in the control room when we left,' said Jolie, casting a worried glance in its direction. The two-man rescue team were nowhere to be seen, though it was obvious from their tracks that they'd made it to the tower.

By the time they reached the helicopter and Abe had sat Cole down and shone a torch in his eyes, and put it down only to start poking away at Cole's skull, the other rescue team was heading back to the helicopter. They didn't dawdle. Nor did they check the gondola station.

'They're not looking,' said Jolie in a small voice that was at odds with her bulky, double-coat clad frame, and beanie and ski goggles that perched atop her head. Maybe she thought the ragged attire detracted from her beauty. Someone ought to tell her it didn't, thought Cole grimly. 'They're not even turning their heads.'

Abe said nothing. Jolie looked to Cole next but Cole had no answers for her, either.

The two men reached the helicopter and for a moment said nothing. Cole looked to Jolie, with her arms wrapped tightly around her waist and her face set, her eyes fixed unwaveringly on the first of the would-be rescuers who'd returned empty-handed.

'He's there,' said the first man quietly, glancing at Jolie but returning his attention to Abe. 'He's dead.'

Abe took it hard. The hands examining the gash in Cole's head trembled until finally the older man withdrew them altogether.

Jolie took it hard too. Cole didn't know what Hare had been to her but she closed her eyes and stood utterly still. She said nothing, nothing at all.

'How?' he asked rustily, for some part of his brain still functioned as a ski-field owner's brain should function—seeking the reason for the loss of life of someone in his employ.

'There are no marks on him,' said the first man. 'His clothes are dry and the room is not cold. Hypothermia didn't get him. Best guess is he suffered a heart attack. But it's only a guess.'

Cole nodded. 'Thanks.' The police would need to be informed, and Hare's next of kin. Hare had a daughter somewhere on the north island. Hare's wife had died years ago.

'We'd best get you to the hospital,' said Abe, first to break the heavy silence.

'No hospital,' said Cole.

'You hit your head pretty hard, son,' said Abe gruffly. 'The pair of you crashed to the ground in a gondola, hiked to safety through a blizzard, and I can guarantee if that was what you were wearing you'll have suffered some degree of hypothermia along the way. What gives you the impression you have a choice?'

'No,' said Jolie to the doctor for the umpteenth time. 'There's really no need for me to get undressed. Nothing's broken, nothing's frozen, nothing hurts, and I'm keeping my clothes *on*.' Belligerence wasn't a natural state for Jolie—it took effort and made her tremble, but better that than a full physical. 'You've checked fingers and toes, taken my temperature, and I don't have concussion. Just tell me where to sign so I can get out of here.'

'You can go just as soon as you lie back on the table and let me check your abdomen and your spine. *Through* your clothes if you insist.'

'I insist.'

'You know, belligerence is an early sign of hypothermia,' said the doctor sweetly as she gestured yet again for Jolie to lie down on the examination table.

'Belligerence is something of a natural state for Jolie,'

said a deep voice from the doorway and there stood Cole Rees and beside him her mother.

Jolie took a step forward, and then she was in her mother's arms and holding on tight. No words for the complex relationship between mother and daughter who'd only really ever had each other, for Jolie's father had died when Jolie was still a baby. Rachel squeezed tighter, before pulling back to study Jolie worriedly. 'You okay, baby?'

'Fine,' said Jolie, close to choking.

'I'd like to believe her,' said the doctor. 'Stand there and let me prod your abdomen and your spine. If you can stay upright, I promise you I'm done.'

Rachel stepped back, and Jolie let the ER doctor do her job as Cole Rees looked on from the doorway. He sported a fresh bandage for the cut on his forehead, and a new overcoat. Maybe he'd borrowed it. Hopefully it was dry.

He looked tired. Battered. And far too appealing for his own good or Jolie's. 'Why are you here?' she asked curtly, spearing him with an unfriendly gaze.

'I tried to teach her some manners, I swear,' said Rachel, frowning at her daughter. Jolie scowled back.

'Guess they didn't take,' murmured Cole. 'I'm checking out. I wanted to make sure you were okay before I left. No ulterior motive, Jolie. Just common courtesy.'

As requested.

She could not hold his gaze. The unspoken words hung in the air as the doctor finished her examination and told Jolie she could go.

Home, *finally*, to where a hot shower waited and getting undressed didn't mean that a physician would know from the scent on her and the state of her underwear that

Jolie Tanner had recently had sex. No one need know about that.

No one.

'I'll walk you and your mother to your car,' Cole said next.

'There's really no need.'

Cole's gaze clashed with hers, his will a living thing. 'Humour me,' he said.

Jolie humoured him, but Cole could tell she wanted him gone. Out of her sight, out of her life, and he would be. Soon. Just as soon as they made their way past the press mob waiting outside the hospital doors. He hadn't mentioned them to Jolie yet.

Rachel didn't mention them, either, although she must've seen them on her way in.

Jolie stopped when she saw them. Stopped and turned as if to flee, only there was no escaping the press when they wanted a piece of a person. Cole knew this for fact.

'Better just to get it over with,' he murmured, and for a fleeting moment he saw terror in her eyes; a fear wholly at odds with the bravery she'd shown on the mountain.

'Isn't there another way out?' she said.

'They'll still find you.' With his hand to the small of her back, he urged her forwards, nothing untoward, but she trembled anyway and he didn't think it was with desire. 'We practised this story, remember? I'm not going to deviate from it, if that's what you're thinking.'

'I really don't think I can do this.' Terror in her gaze, along with a distrust that cut at him.

'Sorry, Red. You don't have a choice.' He glanced at Rachel Tanner. Rachel stared steadily back, her gaze self-assured and slightly mocking. But she'd taken her daughter's hand in her own and didn't look as if she'd be letting it go any time soon. 'Ready?'

And then all three of them stepped outside and it began.

'Mr Rees, can you tell us about the damage sustained up on Silverlake Mountain.'

'Mr Rees, has there been any word on the where-abouts of Hare Robo?'

'Mr Rees, can you tell us why you left your father's funeral to meet with Jolie Tanner?'

'Ms Tanner, can you tell us about the nature of your relationship with Cole Rees?'

'Keep your questions relevant or don't ask them at all,' said Cole, pinning the burly reporter blocking Jolie's way with a flat stare. 'If I may. The avalanche damage to Silverlake is extensive. Ms Tanner and I were both caught in it but sustained only minor injuries. Thank you for your concern. My manager, Hare Robo, was operating the gondola ski-lift service from the control tower at the time the blizzard struck. His whereabouts is currently unknown.'

'Mr Rees, can you give us an estimate of how much it will cost to repair the damages to Silverlake ski field?'

'Not yet.'

'Mr Rees, your sister is quoted as saying that you've been heading up Rees Enterprises for some time now and that your father's death will have little effect on the day-to-day running of Rees Holdings.'

'That's correct.'

'She's also quoted as saying she sees no reason why

you and Miss Tanner would have arranged to meet on the mountain on the day of your father's funeral.'

'Also correct.'

'But you *do* have a cabin up there.' The swarthy reporter shot Rachel an oily smile and she lifted a bored and quizzical brow in reply. Jolie shrank back against his arm, her trembling twofold. 'A cabin your father used to use regularly to conduct…*business*.'

'Of course.'

'So what were you and Ms Tanner *doing* up there?'

'Speaking for myself, I was saying goodbye to my father,' said Cole grimly. 'I took the last gondola ride back down the mountain. So did Ms Tanner. Then the avalanche struck and knocked me unconscious. When I came to I couldn't tell sky from snow. Ms Tanner got me back up the mountain to safety. She did it in sub-zero temperatures in the middle of a blizzard by hauling herself and occasionally me through a nightmare landscape. I owe her my life. I owe her my thanks. And I extend to her my wholehearted admiration for her determination, quick thinking and mountain craft. Have I made myself clear?'

No juicy scandal in any of that, and the burly reporter knew it.

'Ms Tanner, do *you* have any comment?' he said with an insincere smile.

'No,' said Jolie, and if the word came out thready it was only because she had no defences left. Not against the press of people staring at her so avidly. Not against Cole.

He'd heard her. All those awful things she'd said to him about the way his father's actions had coloured her life. Cole had listened.

He'd said he admired her—out loud and in public, a Rees had praised a Tanner. It didn't compute, the same way his arm at her back making her feel safe didn't compute.

'You must have *some* comment,' said the persistent reporter, as if to have none was unthinkable.

'I'm glad I'm alive,' she said raggedly. 'I'm glad Cole is. And I'm absolutely beat and just want to go home. Those are my comments.'

Cole looked at the reporter. The reporter looked at Cole. 'Move,' said Cole softly. And then they were through the throng and Cole dropped his arm and walked them to Rachel's car.

'You did fine back there,' he said with a searching green-eyed gaze as Rachel headed for the driver's side door.

Jolie nodded and looked away.

'I wouldn't have fed you to them, Jolie,' he said next. 'That's not my way.'

She ended up shrugging, because she had no answer to give him. 'Now I know that.'

'Not exactly trusting, are you?'

'No.' She'd never had cause to be. 'I don't know what I expected back there,' she said quietly. 'Not that. Not your support. Not your thanks. I—thank you.'

'I'll try not to make a habit of it if it rattles you so much.'

'You do that.'

He shook his head, his smile a curious mixture of appreciation and regret. And then he turned and strode away.

'Nice of him,' offered Rachel mildly as they got into the car, and Jolie tried not to stare at Cole as he made his way towards the waiting taxi. Where was his family? Were they so adamant about not wanting to be seen anywhere near a Tanner that they hadn't even come to collect him from the hospital? What kind of a family was that?

'What did you make of him?' asked Rachel, into Jolie's continued silence.

'I thought…' she said and lapsed into contemplation as Rachel reversed the car out of the car park and pulled away. 'I thought he was amazing. He never gave up. Not once. He always got back up.'

Not everyone had, up there on the mountain. Not everyone had survived. Jolie took a shuddering breath.

'Hare's dead. They think he had a heart attack. He said—' Jolie tried to blink away the rapidly forming tears but this time they wouldn't stay back. 'He said to tell you he was sorry for your loss. He wanted me to make sure I said it right.'

This time, when the tears came, Jolie made no move to stop them.

CHAPTER FIVE

A DAY made a difference. Two days made more.

Two days and Jolie had her emotions under control enough to join her mother behind the bar in the evenings, and draw beers and talk half pipes and diamond runs with the best of them. On the subject of her time on the mountain with Cole Rees, she remained firmly recalcitrant. A smile, a quip and a change of subject worked well. If that didn't work, she then talked about watching the avalanche up close from the gondola, just before it crashed to the ground.

That tended to shut them up. That tended to produce wide-eyed shudders all round.

Not a big establishment, Rachel's Bar. More of a long skinny hole in the wall with outstanding wine and liquor lists, boutique beer on tap, and a Polynesian chef called Ophelia-Anne in charge of the kitchen. No one sauced seafood like Ophelia-Anne. No one ever ran a kitchen quite like her, either. The menu was a blackboard one and changed daily. Dishes were rarely repeated. And when Ophelia-Anne wasn't there, the bar did not serve food.

The kitchen was open this evening, and the room overflowing with a mix of locals who'd heard Ophelia-Anne was slow roasting salmon, and tourists who wanted somewhere cosy to sit and something decent to drink.

This bar had started out as Rachel's challenge. An inappropriate project to take her mind off her equally inappropriate dalliance with a married man. Somewhere along the way it had become Rachel's solace. A warm place. A place where Rachel Tanner held her head high and became a whole lot more than Rees's mistress.

He'd come in here more and more towards the end, James Rees. To spend time with Rachel and to eat Ophelia-Anne's food and to hell with the gossip and the trouble it had caused. He'd got careless. That or he'd just stopped giving a damn about being discreet.

Jolie had never seen *Cole* Rees in the bar.

Until now.

Rachel had seen him come in—no way she hadn't. But she left him for Jolie to serve.

'Cole. What can I get you?' Jolie was politeness itself as she pushed a drinks list towards him.

'I'm not here to drink, Jolie.' From the barely leashed anger in his voice he wasn't here to socialise, either.

'Then let me rephrase,' she said evenly. 'What do you want?'

'Doesn't matter, does it? I'm here to give you this.' He placed a document envelope on the bar in front of her. 'My father provided for you in his will. Your mother too. Any halfway decent solicitor will know what to do to complete the transfers. Alternatively, if there's something you don't understand about the documents, you could always try returning one of my calls.'

He nodded to Rachel. He spared Jolie one more seething glance.

And then he left.

Jolie picked up the envelope and tapped it thoughtfully against the polished mahogany bar. Heavy envelope. Plenty in it. Cole's animosity piqued her interest. She'd thought…well, they were never going to be friends but she'd thought they'd come to a better understanding of one another up on that mountainside. She'd thought they'd carved out some measure of tolerance for each other.

Guess not.

Something had obviously happened to change his mind. Something to do with his father's will.

Sighing, she retreated to a corner of Ophelia-Anne's kitchen and pulled out the sheaf of papers, and started by reading the letter at the front. A letter from James's legal people.

'What did Cole want?' asked Rachel from the doorway a few minutes later.

'Probably to strangle me,' said Jolie slowly as she flicked through the papers one more time to be sure. 'He said he's been leaving messages for me to call him, but my phone's not working right. Hasn't been for days, ever since the avalanche. I'll have to get a new one. Anyway, not important. They've read James's will. Cole's the executor. It seems James has left me a house in Christchurch and a harbourside apartment in Auckland.'

'Foolish man.' But Rachel didn't seem surprised. 'I told him not to.'

'You *knew*?'

'I knew he wanted to do *something* for you. He wasn't unaware of how hard you had it sometimes, on account of his relationship with me.'

Jolie closed her eyes and shook her head. 'Pity he

couldn't have *legitimised* his relationship with you,' she muttered, and earned herself a sharp glance from Ophelia-Anne. 'What do I want with a house and an apartment?'

'Financial security?' countered Rachel dryly. 'Somewhere other than a dogbox to live?'

'It's a very nice dogbox,' muttered Jolie. 'What's more, *I* pay the rent. I make my own way, Mama. You know that. You *taught* me that.'

'I know,' said Rachel. 'I told him that. But the man had it in his head to make amends.'

'Yeah, well, he left you something too,' said Jolie. 'And, boy, was he making amends.' Maybe he was planning to *buy* his way into heaven.

Rachel had unfolded her arms. Her chin came up, her grey eyes flashed. 'James left me nothing. I didn't want anything. We agreed.'

'Seems he changed his mind. He left you a share portfolio worth sixteen million.' Jolie shoved the papers back into the envelope and slapped it into her mother's hands as she squeezed past her on her way back out to the bar. 'Not dollars. Sixteen million pounds.'

The Rees Holdings office complex favoured function over form, but Cole's office still commanded a respectable view and the room had all the things needed to make visitors feel as if they were dealing with someone suitably important. That his sister, Hannah, chose to barge into his office with only a peremptory warning knock surprised no one, least of all Cole. That she proceeded to talk about the stipulations their father had placed in his will did surprise him. Hannah could usually command a whole lot more discretion than this. Not to mention common sense.

'You really want to contest our father's will?' he said, when finally she paused for breath. 'Because I can assure you, Hannah, it's airtight. Our father wasn't a stupid man. Just a wilful one.'

But Hannah wouldn't be appeased. Instead she turned tragic eyes on him, and let forth another impassioned tirade against Rachel and Jolie Tanner, culminating in a declaration that she couldn't stand the thought of just how *much* those whores must've bled their father over the years.

Cole, who'd spent the last two days discovering just how much Rachel Tanner *hadn't* taken from his father, figured it was time to share those particular findings, even if it wasn't likely to bring on the joy.

'They took nothing, Hannah. Not that I can see. You can go through the financials yourself if you like. My guess is that every time James wanted to give Rachel Tanner a gift and she refused him, he added to the share portfolio he started for her over twelve years ago. She just didn't know it.'

'Oh, she knew, all right.' Hannah seethed in spectacular fashion; a bejewelled little dragon on the hunt for someone to scorch. 'Cole, she *knew*.'

'Suit yourself.' Cole didn't waste his breath trying to convince Hannah otherwise. It didn't matter what his sister thought. It didn't matter what anyone thought. 'Look, Hannah. The money was never a part of the company structure to begin with. It's always been separate. Before this week you never even knew it was *there*.'

'You are *not* giving it to them,' said Hannah fiercely.

'I already have, and before you start ranting I have a few suggestions for you. Stop obsessing about the Tanner women. Stop idolising a father who never deserved it, and start thinking about whether you want to take up the directorship I've offered you in Sydney. You'd be good at it and you need to get away from this place and the memories it holds for you. It's not healthy. You're turning into a replica of our mother, only more twisted.'

'Oh, I am, am I?' she shot back. 'And since when have you been so holier than thou? You hate what Rachel Tanner did to our family, Cole. I know you do.'

'Maybe she was just a catalyst. Maybe we created a family full of rifts all by ourselves. And maybe it's time we stopped.' Cole took a breath and regarded his sister speculatively. She was twenty-five and to his knowledge had never had a serious relationship. She held a University Blue in Business Studies. She had another first-class degree in Arts, majoring in psychology. That she'd ended up such a right royal basket case of conflicting emotions, beginning with abandonment issues and ending with hate for all things Tanner, was entirely his father's fault and just one more reason to curse the man to the depths of hell. Credit where credit was due. 'Ethan Carter wants to transfer home from Sydney. I could use him here. I could use you there. What am I going to tell him?'

'You want me gone,' said Hannah, shooting him a sharp green glance from eyes so very like his own. 'Why?'

'I want you happy,' said Cole quietly. 'Is that so wrong?'

'You're different,' she said finally. 'Since the mountain. You brood more. Work harder than ever. What happened up there, Cole?'

'Nothing you'd want to know about.'

'But I *do* want to know.'

'I saw nature move a mountain. I realised my own insignificance. I watched a woman refuse to give up on me and on herself. I survived. What else would you like to know?'

'She was brave?' said Hannah with a catch in her voice.

'She has a name, Hannah. She was your closest friend once. And, yes, Jolie was brave, and determined, and annoying, and resourceful, and then when we got back to Queenstown the attention from the press terrified her and she thought I was going to feed her to them.' Cole threw his pen down on the table. 'You want to know how *small* I felt at that particular moment in time? How *angry* I was with her for thinking I would do that? How furious I was with my father and his adultery, and myself for not being someone Jolie felt she could trust, and even with you for turning your back on her all those years ago. She trusts no one, Han. No one even gets close.'

Hannah bit her lip. 'I had to break that friendship, Cole. The situation...'

'I know.' Caution warring with the need for truth. 'I want to see her again, Han.'

'What for?'

'Maybe I want to get close.'

The conversation was all downhill from there.

Hannah did not agree to the Sydney transfer. Hannah pitched a fit. She also threatened to (a) vote against him in all subsequent shareholder meetings, (b) replace him

as CEO the minute she had the numbers, and (c) render
him a eunuch if he so much as went *near* Jolie Tanner.
Not necessarily in that order.

Just before she stormed out she told him that if he had
any feelings for his family whatsoever he should take
two blondes to bed and call her when he got his libido
under control and his brain back in his head.

Derek Haynes, Cole's second-in-command, entered
Cole's office shortly after Hannah's spectacular exit.
Derek didn't bother knocking, either. He did, however,
manage to shut the door behind him.

'Problems?' he said, forgoing a chair.

'Since when has Hannah ever *not* been a problem?'
murmured Cole. 'She's as spoiled and as temperamental
as they come. My father indulged her every whim. Does
she seriously expect me to do the same?'

Derek raised an eyebrow. Derek looked wholly
amused. 'Yes. Speaking of which, if you're planning
on any more shouting matches may I suggest somewhere
a little more private? Walls are thin, Cole. There's now
an office pool on who those blondes might be or an
alternative vote that it's going to be a redhead.'

'Which way did you vote?'

'I need more data before committing. Why do you
think I'm here?'

'I was hoping you had the latest estimate on the
Silverlake clean-up.'

'I sent it through five minutes ago, despot. Check
your emails.'

Cole checked and there it was. He opened Derek's
spreadsheet and swore.

'We've been friends a long time, Cole,' said Derek,
and Cole narrowed his gaze. In six years of working

together and five years of university before that, Derek had *never* played the friendship card. 'I don't usually question your judgement.'

'You can get to the point any time now,' said Cole.

'All right, I will. Frankly, I don't care who you take to your bed and neither does anyone else in your admin staff. You never bed anyone working for you and it has never yet impacted on Rees Holdings. It's just food for gossip.'

'Is this supposed to be reassuring?'

'Just giving you the opinion on the floor.'

'Just get on with it.'

'Fine. Those restructuring plans you have before the board—you need Hannah's vote to push them through. Selling the Australian cotton acreage to finance the Silverlake rebuild—you'll need her vote for that too. Bringing the Shore Hotel refurb in under budget—that's Hannah's baby. The Day Spas are in your mother's care and their profit margin boggles the mind. Hannah and Christina won't be able to pull the votes together to oust you, Cole, but you still need their co-operation, and if you think you can take up with a Tanner woman and not have them go completely mental, think again. That's how they lost James. They are *not* going to take kindly to losing you there too. They'll fight you with everything they have.'

'My father managed to secure their co-operation.'

'You're not your father.'

CHAPTER SIX

IT WAS Cole's second funeral in a week, only this time he wasn't sitting in a front-row pew. That debatable honour went to Hare's daughter and her husband and their offspring, three tousle-haired teenage sons who'd joined their grandfather during school holidays for too many years to count. Handsome boys with the promise of their grandfather's size and the wisdom of their grandfather's words deeply ingrained in them. Cole sought the family out once the service was over.

No one had been on the mountain since the night of the blizzard. There'd been more snow. The area was high risk and likely to stay that way for quite some time.

'Soon,' he murmured when Hare's daughter had asked him when they could get up there. 'As soon as it's safe we'll get up there. I know it's a priority to have Hare's stuff brought down.' So many priorities these days, demanding his time. There'd be an insurance payout too. Hare had died on the job. Cole had lodged the paperwork already. 'I'm sorry for your loss.' Such comfortless words, but he didn't have any others. 'We're going to miss Hare here too. Silverlake won't be the same without him.'

More words, and none of them enough. There were

a great many Silverlake employees in attendance and Cole went out of his way to speak with them. He'd already slotted all of Silverlake's permanent staff within other Rees businesses. He'd managed to find positions for almost half of Silverlake's casual staff at various ski resorts—hauling in favours and getting them to the top of employment wait lists. The rest of the casuals he'd kept on payroll because he'd need them once clean-up began. Silverlake was unlikely to reopen this season, and everybody knew it.

Jolie and Rachel Tanner were at the funeral too. Jolie, glowing and glorious in a subdued funeral dress and elegant black coat. Aloof. Unapproachable.

Breathtaking.

He managed to avoid her. He managed not to stare at her too much. He knew he shouldn't do what he was thinking of doing. For one thing, he didn't have the time.

It had been a tough working week and there were plenty more to come. Company confidence had taken a hit, what with James's death and the happenings at Silverlake. Hannah, bless her self-serving heart, had eventually seen the need to present a united front and was backing his decisions all the way and working just as hard as Cole to minimise the damage done.

So many good reasons not to go after Jolie Tanner, beginning with his responsibility to the family companies and ending with a responsibility to his sister and mother, and Jolie too, when it came to not dragging their names through a river of old mud.

Cole wasn't always honest with his feelings. Sometimes they shamed him. His conflicting feelings for his parents, both living and dead. His conflicting emotions as a teenager for a tiny redheaded waif with eyes too big for her face and a stain on her reputation that just wouldn't go away.

He'd *known*, even then, that she hadn't deserved either his ire or the gossip that had swirled around her. She'd made very few friends after Hannah had abandoned her. She'd kept to herself. Developed a wariness a mile wide. Boys had fallen for Jolie by the truckload throughout her teens, but precious few had earned her favour and the rare youth she *had* gone out with had been close-mouthed and oddly defensive about her afterwards.

Dig past the myth of Jolie Tanner, boyfriend-stealer, and there was a woman in there with courage and fortitude and a will that had got him up that damned mountain and kept him from freezing. A woman with issues and insecurities and vulnerabilities that made *him* feel raw because of the part he'd played in putting them there.

Cole stood his ground as she murmured something to her mother and headed towards him with a dancer's grace that hadn't been in evidence on the mountain. Different clothes. Different shoes.

How he'd ever mistaken that face for a boy's was beyond him.

Her bruises had faded, that or make-up concealed them. A rueful smile lent a winsome curve to that full and kissable mouth. He hadn't forgotten. Not her mouth. Not the rest of her. He wished to hell he had.

'My mother said you'd be here,' she murmured. 'I wasn't so sure.'

'You should have been.'

'It was a nice ceremony,' she said next, as if small talk

could ease the sting of her barb and the unaccountable hurt he'd taken from it.

'Yes.'

'We're having a wake back at the bar after the burial. There's no pressure on you to join us, but you're invited,' she said next.

'You finally going to buy me that drink, Red?'

'That's a very bad idea.'

'So people keep saying.'

'Maybe you should listen to them.'

'I do. You came over to me, Red. I didn't single you out. I didn't cut at you by implying that you didn't have enough respect for Hare to turn up for his funeral. I didn't do a damn thing.'

Anger in him, and startled surprise from her.

'I'm sorry,' she said as a blush stained her cheeks. 'For the crack about you not attending Hare's funeral. I knew someone would be here to represent the Rees family. I think I knew all along it would be you.' She took a ragged breath. 'Maybe I just didn't want it to be.'

'You're wounding me, Red. Again.'

Frowning, Jolie looked away.

'Are you sleeping?' he asked gruffly. 'You look tired.'

'So do you.' But she didn't look at him as she said it.

'Lots to do.'

'Yes. Yes, I heard you'd been finding jobs for all the Silverlake employees. It's very good of you.'

'Aren't you going to attribute me with an ulterior motive?'

'No,' she said quietly, and their eyes met and Cole's breath lodged somewhere in his chest. 'No, I don't think I am. As for me not sleeping, I can hardly blame my work for that because I've barely been doing any. I've been having bad dreams. Nightmares, about falling.'

'In the gondola?'

'Yes. There's usually a bottle of champagne floating around in mid-air too, in my dreams. And for some unknown reason a box full of kitchen knives. And a potato masher. They tend to go all matrix on me. It's very disconcerting.'

'I can imagine,' he said. 'Knives haven't featured in any of my dreams.'

'Lucky you.'

'Not really. Ask me what I dream of, Jolie. Ask me where I go when I close my eyes at night.'

'I'm not sure I want to know.'

Wary, and so she should be, given the chaos she caused in him. Cole stepped in close and bent his head so that his lips brushed the hair at her temple. 'Thank you for the invitation to the wake. I'd like to attend for a while. Thank you for coming over to speak to me, even if civility's a stretch. And just for the record, when I close my eyes at night I think of greedy lips and silken skin and blinding passion the likes of which I've *never* felt before. Ask me where I go each night, Red.'

Grey eyes, wide and startled. A mouth made for kisses; not one kiss but more.

'Where?' she whispered and it was a supplicant's murmur and it magnified the heat deep inside him a hundredfold.

'I come to you.'

* * *

'Drinks are on the house,' said Jolie some two hours later as she handed the one remaining whiskey neat on her tray to the silver-tongued and dangerously appealing Cole Rees. 'This isn't from me.'

'Thank you for explaining,' he said with the hint of a smile in his eyes that wasn't at odds with the mood in the room. Wakes didn't have to be gloomy affairs and this one was shaping up to be anything but. Someone had brought along an old photo album and several of the pictures had Hare in them. There was a story for each one. A toast for each story. And so it went.

Emboldened by her familiar surroundings, Jolie let her gaze linger on Cole's lips. The smile in his eyes was mirrored there too, and it was a wry thing with too much charm in it for comfort. No wonder women flocked to him and took whatever crumbs he offered. He had the money, he knew how to ratchet up a woman's desire, and, above all, he had the touch.

Dear Lord, he had an easy touch.

'You were saying?' he murmured, and Jolie felt her cheeks turn warm as she wrenched her gaze away from those lips and back to his eyes.

'No, I was thinking,' she corrected. 'Mainly about what you said before. I think,' she offered carefully, 'that maybe it was just the circumstances up on the mountain that made what we did seem so…extraordinary. Heightened awareness due to a near-death experience and all that.'

'It's a valid theory,' he murmured. 'Care to test it?'

'Not really, no.'

'Why not? All I'm asking for is a kiss.'

'Happens I've heard that line before,' she said, and

bailed on the conversation by simple dint of heading back to the bar to load up her tray with more drinks.

When she glanced back, Cole Rees was watching her. What was more, he was smiling.

'Is Cole Rees here for the wake or for you?' asked Rachel during one of the lulls behind the bar.

'The wake,' said Jolie. 'But let's just assume for the moment that he might be here for me. How do I get rid of him?'

'Have you tried ignoring him?'

'He's too annoying to ignore.'

Rachel's eyebrows rose.

'Well, he is,' muttered Jolie.

'Have you tried running?'

'You usually tell me not to run.'

'Depends on the threat,' murmured Rachel.

'I've also tried pushing him away, but that's not working too well, either. Apparently he *likes* being insulted.'

'I doubt it,' said Rachel dryly. 'No, what he *likes* is that you're playing hard to get.'

'I *am* hard to get,' said Jolie irritably.

Rachel handed Jolie an empty tray to fill and nodded in the direction of the crowd. 'Hence the challenge.'

'My mother seems to think that if I simper at you, you'll go away,' Jolie said to Cole the next time he found himself free of fawning admirers.

'She could be right,' he said amiably. 'Give it a try.'

Scowling, Jolie strode away and this time he didn't just grin at her retreating back, he laughed.

* * *

The next time they spoke, he was the one to initiate the conversation. 'My solicitor hasn't heard anything back on that paperwork I gave you,' he said.

'That's because it's still sitting on top of the egg rack in Ophelia-Anne's kitchen.'

'Why?'

'Ever heard of the too-hard basket?' she murmured.

'Yes, but I've never put sixteen million pounds in it before,' he countered. 'Give or take a dwelling or two.'

'I did *not* know about those houses,' she said in a fierce undertone. 'I don't *want* them.'

'So you say,' he said. 'But if that's honestly how you feel, you still have to decide what else to do with them.'

'Can't I just refuse them and you keep them?'

But Cole just smiled faintly. 'Sorry, that's not how it works. Get a solicitor, Jolie. It's the best advice I can give you.'

'Your mother must be—' Jolie stopped abruptly.

'The word you're looking for is *shamed*,' said Cole. 'Hannah's incensed. I just want the paperwork off my plate.'

'You're not resentful?'

'I'm *very* resentful,' muttered Cole. 'Mainly because my esteemed father waited until after he was dead to acknowledge just how much he cared for your mother, and left me to deal with the fallout.'

'What else did he leave you?' asked Jolie in a very small voice. 'He wouldn't have forgotten you. He was too proud of you.'

'I hold forty per cent of the company shares. It's

what I wanted. Hannah controls a significant stake too, although whether she wants it is anyone's guess. My mother has always been a company shareholder. Now she holds more. Property-wise, there was plenty to go around. James provided enough for everyone. Some of us just have to work harder than others in order to keep it.'

'How much is it going to cost to reopen Silverlake?' she asked hesitantly, and Cole rubbed at his temple with the heel of his hand in the way of tired little boys who could no longer think straight.

'A lot,' he muttered. 'I'm on it.'

'Maybe you should get off it for the night,' said Jolie. 'You want another drink?'

'No. I want—'

'Food? Ophelia-Anne's got platters coming out.'

'I want to get out of here,' he said, his voice low and rough. 'With you. And before you tell me yet again that this is a very bad idea, I know.'

'Then why do it?'

'Maybe I'm hoping it'll get you out of my system.'

'And if it doesn't?'

'Then all hell breaks loose.' He looked beyond weary. Past patience. And very, very appealing. 'Are you coming or not?'

Maybe it was the brutal honesty of his words that got to her. And maybe there was just something about a man who ran scorching hot beneath his surface calm.

'All right.' Jolie rubbed at her wrist with the thumb of her other hand, a nervous gesture and he knew it for such, but he didn't call her on it. He just watched, and waited. 'Give me another hour here to get the food out and bring someone else in to cover for me. Then I'll get my coat.'

Cole's car was an engineering marvel with an interior of unbridled luxury. Jolie settled into the leather seat and let reality as she knew it slip soundlessly away. Jolie didn't even own a car. 'Where are we going?'

'My place.'

'Can there be ice cream?'

'If you like.'

They got ice cream from a specialty store in the city. And then he took her home.

Cole's split-level home on the outskirts of Queenstown was a lot like his car: supremely functional, beautiful and worth plenty. The man lived in comfort: dark leather furniture, miles of gleaming wooden benches and balustrades, sideboards and bookshelves. Ivory wool carpet for toes to sink into, and everything in its place, until Cole got there, that was, and then his coat went over the back of one chair and his jacket claimed a kitchen bench.

A fire had been set in the huge open fireplace; the flick of a match got it started.

'You have a housekeeper,' she said as she set the ice cream they'd purchased on the kitchen counter and shrugged out of her own coat.

'Guilty.'

'One who spoils you,' she added as he returned from his forage through the fridge with a plate of wicked-looking brownies.

'Also true. Her name's Maree and she's been with

the family since before I was born. She's semi-retired. These days she only does my place.'

'Spoiled rotten *and* the family favourite.'

'No, that would be Hannah,' he said without rancour.

But Hannah Rees was not a subject Jolie wanted to dwell on. 'What's it like?' she said as she turned to study the view of the lake from Cole's tall tinted windows. 'Growing up as James Rees's heir? Knowing that one day you'd come into a whole lot of power and responsibility, and wealth. Did it ever go to your head?'

'On occasion,' he said. 'At which point my father would invariably find for me the lowliest holiday job possible in one of our companies, from which I'd return suitably chastened.'

'So what happens now that the power's all yours?' He'd loosened his tie and freed the top button of his white business shirt. He was scooping ice cream on top of brownies. 'Who'll chasten you now?'

'Probably no one,' he said, and the devil was in his smile. 'You can expect arrogance.'

'Is that what your bringing me here is?' she asked. 'A display of arrogance and power? A warning to your family that you'll not be controlled?'

'No,' he said, handing her a plate topped with the ice cream and brownie confection and a spoon to go with it. 'You're not part of any Rees family power play.'

'Are you planning to wreak vengeance on me for the sins of my mother?' she asked next, sliding her spoon through creamy ice cream with double choc and brownie chunks. 'Make me fall in love with you and then cast me aside?'

'No. I told you why I invited you here, Jolie.'

'So you did.' The ice cream was delicious. The brownie was better. 'You want me out of your system. I'd like you out of mine. Here's to making it happen.' Jolie headed for the fire, leaving Cole free to follow. Or not. She didn't know where this was going. The mask she reached for was a brittle one, laden with sarcasm and other mechanisms guaranteed to create distance. 'You have a very beautiful house. Is this where you bring all your women?'

Cole's eyes narrowed. Jolie ignored his silent warning. Naked flame at her back and ice cream sliding down her throat—always a good combination. 'Warm fire, a cosy lounge. I'm betting the bedroom's glorious too.'

'What's your point?'

'I just want to make sure that this is a regular environment for you when it comes to seduction, nothing memorable about it. Me, I'm liking the fire. And the brownie. The luxury's very appealing. Hard to forget. I think you have the purging advantage.'

'You're babbling, Red.' That and amusing the hell out of him, if the smile on his face was any indication.

'Sorry.' And she was. 'It's possible I'm nervous.' More nervous than usual.

Cole's smile grew wider.

'That smile is hardly reassuring,' she told him. 'So what comes next? How do you want to do this?'

'Well, I usually start with sweet talk and compliments, but I think I'd be wasting my time. Besides, I wouldn't want to burden you with anything too memorable.'

Jolie had the sinking suspicion that it was already too late for that. Time to concentrate on her ice cream and brownie, except that Cole stepped in close and took the plate from her hand and set it on the fireplace mantel. Jolie eyed the plate surreptitiously. Then she eyed him.

'Even if you're thinking it, please don't say that you'd rather have the sweets than me,' he murmured. 'That would be memorable. I might even consider it a challenge.'

And then he touched his fingers to the curve of her jaw and parted her lips with the pad of his thumb. He touched his lips to hers. Not a punishment but a gentle thing that demanded little in the way of response.

As far as Jolie was concerned, all it did was whet her already ravenous appetite.

And then Cole smiled and stepped away, and handed her back her plate.

'What was that?' she asked suspiciously.

'That was a kiss,' he offered. 'The beginning of the purge.'

'I really don't think you gave it your all.'

He sent her a deliciously slow smile. 'That's the point.'

'Ah.' She finished the last spoonful of her dessert and set the spoon aside and slid her forefinger through the runny ice cream on the plate. 'You *do* realise that this evening's going to end really, really badly for both of us.'

'I'm counting on it, Red.' Cole's gaze hadn't left her forefinger. Maybe he thought she was going to put on a little show for his benefit. She could have, of course. She could have put her finger to her lips and savoured the texture and taste and watched Cole's gaze darken.

Instead, she touched her finger to *his* lips and waited to see what he would do.

Cole managed some discipline.

He cobbled together at least *some* control as he took her finger in his mouth and tasted what she offered him.

He slid his hands in her hair and kissed her properly after that, and gave in to the desire that had been riding him for days. All in, no holding back, and neither did Jolie, and it was the sleeping bag all over again. Darkness, and sweetness, and a kiss that bordered on reverent as their lips met, and their tongues touched and tangled.

He needed this. He needed *her*. And he didn't know why and he knew it for a bad choice, but he couldn't bring himself to care.

Cole's shirt came off first, Jolie's hurry, not his, for he wasn't done with kissing yet. But he found the zipper of her dress moments later, and there was something to be said for soft creamy shoulders and a woman who looked at a man as if she knew every hidden corner of his soul and accepted him anyway and urged him to take what he would and to hell with the consequences.

The elegant hollow where shoulder met neck. The curve of a breast as he picked her up and carried her to the couch, easing her onto it and him to his knees. Slender legs wide open now. More kisses. More glowing silken skin.

'Is this how you remember it?' she whispered, watching him. A slender flame with a siren's soul.

'No.'

'That's good, right?' As she set her lips to his neck and he flung his head back to allow her better access.

'Right.' He slid his hands along her thighs and beneath her dress. She didn't stop him as he smoothed his hands over the curves of her buttocks and drew her against him. She encouraged him.

It wasn't long before Jolie had his trousers off. Another kiss that threatened to destroy him and Jolie's panties came off too.

'There's something I want from you,' he whispered as tip met silken heat. He watched her face as he slowly eased inside her. Watched her eyes turn blind and sensuality take hold.

'Ask,' she whispered as she arched up into his possession, and then prevented him from doing so by drawing his mouth down to hers. 'Ask.' With a new tension in her voice and in her body as he adjusted the angle of his thrusts in order to rub where rubbing was due.

'This time when you come, you wait for me.'

'Wouldn't it be better if we *didn't* achieve simultaneous earth-shattering release?' she murmured. 'Could be a little too memorable, and we wouldn't want that.'

'Look at it this way.' He skimmed the backs of his fingers across her breast, and when she closed her eyes and gasped he filled his palm and impaled her to the hilt. One hand at her hip now and the other teasing a pebbled nipple as he thrust again, slow and hard. 'You're probably going to hate it.'

'You're right.' Another slow slide and a whimper from Jolie to go with it. 'You are so right. I'm going to hate it.'

'Kiss me,' he whispered, and she did. Just one, but they made it last for ever.

And when he soared he took her with him.

Nights could pass quickly and nights could pass slow. This one took for ever and Jolie savoured every moment. Cole Rees was an enigma but in the bedroom one thing was perfectly clear. He gave more than he demanded and he demanded utter surrender.

He had a fondness for a woman's back and Jolie let him at hers more than once during the night. He loved the slightness of her and the fall of her hair. He demanded patience and then deliberately made her lose it. He had that slow, easy touch but how his mouth made her scream.

And in the cold before dawn when he hardened inside her yet again, this time he used his mouth to tell her she was killing him.

'I've seen you half dead,' she murmured as she eased him onto his back and made love to him with a patience she'd only recently learned. 'And this isn't it.'

Moments later he proved her right.

The next time Jolie woke she was in a king-sized bed with snow-white sheets, a crimson duvet draped half over her, sunlight streaming in through gauze-covered windows and not an ebony-haired green-eyed lover in sight.

He wasn't in the shower, either, although that didn't stop Jolie from enjoying it, or the divinely scented shower gel that she applied liberally to her body. She'd gone to Cole's bed willingly. To slake a need, she told herself. To try and figure out exactly what *had* happened up there on the mountain. To see if it would happen again.

Boy, had it happened again.

So much for purging.

She finished showering and dried herself off. She donned yesterday's dress and applied what little make-up she had in her purse and tried not to worry too much about what might happen next.

Cole wasn't in the living room.

He wasn't in the kitchen.

His housekeeper, on the other hand, was.

The erstwhile Maree took one look at Jolie, closed her eyes and muttered a very ungrandmotherly curse. Alas, when she opened her eyes again, Jolie was still there. Halfway into her coat and looking for the nearest exit, mind, but very definitely present, and very definitely someone Cole's housekeeper hadn't been expecting to see.

'I'm guessing you'd rather we skip the introductions,' said Jolie with far more insouciance than she felt. 'I, ah…' Jolie couldn't seem to find the sleeve of her coat. 'Is Cole about?'

'No.'

'No as in he's not in the house at all? Or no as in he's not in this room?'

'It's twenty past eleven. Cole's at work.' Maree's lips stretched thin and flat once she'd spoken the words. 'He said to let you sleep.'

'Good of him.' Jolie finally found her other coat sleeve. 'What else did he say?'

'Nothing.' Maree was rolling out some kind of pastry dough. Maree's pastry was unlikely to be melt-in-your-mouth flaky today. Nor did Maree seem inclined towards any sort of hospitality whatsoever. 'Nothing at all.'

'Any coffee around?'

'No.'

'How about tea?'

Maree's glare was a good match for her lips. Humourless and thin.

'How about a pen and some notepaper?'

'Sorry. We're all out.'

'All right,' said Jolie grimly, in the face of such outstanding hospitality. 'Last question, I promise. Are *you* going to call for a cab to collect Jolie Tanner from Cole Rees's house or am I?'

CHAPTER SEVEN

COLE didn't know what had possessed him to flee his own house, leaving Jolie fast asleep in his bed.

He told himself she probably wouldn't have expected him to stay seeing as it was a weekday and all and he had to go to work.

He almost convinced himself that he'd left without waking her on account of her recent bout of sleepless nights. Courteous to a fault, that was him.

He tried to ignore the head-spinning fear that had lodged in him upon waking up this morning. The sickening sensation that in bedding Jolie again he'd somehow just made the biggest mistake of his life.

Everything he'd ever wanted, from the fiercest pleasure to bone-deep contentment—she'd given it. Unbridled eroticism caked in beauty and desire. No need had gone unmet, not one, and as for purging himself of her, or gorging himself so as to kill his appetite for her, clearly the joke was on him.

He couldn't stop thinking about her. All he wanted was more of her.

He'd come in to work so that he wouldn't simply turn around and offer her whatever the hell she wanted from him; that was how besotted he was with one Jolie Tanner.

Cole heard no knocking but the door to his office opened anyway to admit Hannah carrying a folder full of yet more papers to add to the ones already on his desk. One of these days Hannah was going to relearn the fine art of knocking. Hopefully it wouldn't take long. She would never have dreamed of barging into their late father's office unannounced.

'I need to speak to you about the Shore Hotel refurb,' she said abruptly.

'I'm listening.'

'I can't bring it in under budget.'

'Why not?'

'The plumber says that the water pipes in the heritage wing are leaching lead. They have to be replaced.'

'Didn't you account for that in the original estimate?'

'No.'

Cole closed his eyes.

'I overlooked it, all right?' said Hannah tightly.

'All right.' Cole opened his eyes and regarded his sister steadily. 'How much is it going to cost?'

'I've cut back where I could in other areas. Some of the more expensive furnishings can wait.'

'Hannah, how much?'

'Another three point two million.'

Not chump change. Not the kind of refurbishment he or anyone else had had in mind. He eyed the folder in Hannah's hand with resignation. 'Those the new figures?'

'Yes.'

'Leave them here. I'll take a look and then pass them on to Derek. You can pick them up from him.'

'Cole, I'm sorry. I know we don't need the added expense at the moment. I should have made more allowance for the age of the building and the potential extra costs. I should have *known*.'

'And now you do.' Cole bit back a far harsher retort. 'Anything else?'

'Yes, what have you done to Maree?'

'Maree?' Nothing. Nothing except tell her he had company this morning and not to wake her. He hadn't mentioned names. Possibly a mistake. 'Why?'

'She called earlier to say she'd gone home early, she wanted to retire, and that you need to find yourself a new housekeeper. She sounded upset.'

'Is that so?' he muttered grimly.

'Hey, this one's not my fault,' said Hannah. 'I'm just the messenger.'

'Message received.'

'What are you going to do?' asked Hannah next.

'About finding you another three million for your refurb? I don't know yet.' He'd been over the entire assortment of Rees companies already, with a view to cutting costs and picking up the slack. There was no slack left to pick up. 'You're going to have to leave it with me.'

'I meant about Maree,' said Hannah. 'You want me to talk to her? See if I can find out what's wrong?'

'No. My problem. I'll fix it.'

When Cole returned home that evening, Maree's neatly handwritten resignation was lying flat on the kitchen counter and there were no sweet treats either on the counter or in the fridge. Maree had washed her hands of him on account of his liaison with Jolie Tanner.

Yes, he was listening. Bad Cole.

Not Bad James for committing adultery with Jolie's mother in the first place. Maree certainly hadn't felt obliged to quit her job over *that*. She'd worn that. Soldiered on.

Different standards for different people, apparently. Or perhaps Maree had simply had enough of all of the Rees family intrigues and scandals. The result was the same regardless. No housekeeper. No Jolie. And a decidedly out of sorts Cole.

Quite an achievement, he thought, that, over the course of a ten-hour working day, he'd come up with any number of objections to continuing a relationship with Jolie Tanner and then managed to discard each and every one of them.

His family's disapproval—clearly he took after his father when it came to emotional selfishness, because right now Cole didn't give a damn whether his sister or his mother approved of his relationship with Jolie or not.

The smooth running of the company demanded all his attention—it certainly seemed to at the moment, but Cole's long-term plans involved a healthy work-recreation balance. There would be plenty of room in his life for a woman. She just had to be the *right* woman.

Jolie's elusiveness—this objection had lasted longer than the others, in that, for all Jolie's generosity when it came to sharing her body with him last night, her mind and her heart had remained off limits. She didn't trust easy. She didn't trust *him*, and by leaving her alone in his bed this morning without so much as a goodbye and a hostile housekeeper to deal with when she woke up, not to mention labelling last night nothing more than an attempt to get her out of his system…

Well done, Cole. Seemed he had a few unresolved issues of his own when it came to inviting a woman into his life on even a semi-permanent basis.

Seemed the self-sabotage was alive and well in that regard.

She wasn't even returning his calls.

He reached for a beer, switched the television on to stave off the silence, and stalked through to his bedroom. He shed his clothes, drank half his beer and headed for the ensuite, a white-on-white affair with grey features. He slid the shower door open and blinked. The shower tiles were glossy white. Someone had drawn a large notepad on one of the shower walls using a thick black marker. The notepad had writing on it. Cole's lips began to curve well before he'd finished reading the missive printed thereon.

> *Cole's To Do List*
> *Buy pens and notepaper (according to your housekeeper you don't have any)*
> *Hide pens and notepaper (from housekeeper but where overnight guests can find them)*
> *Define for me the word* Purge. *It does not seem to mean what I think it means.*

Two phone numbers followed. A work number and the mobile number he'd been phoning all day.

Cole strode back into his bedroom, reached for the bedside phone and dialled the mobile number again. This time, Jolie picked up.

'I got your note,' he murmured. 'Where are you?'

'Christchurch. My apartment. I just walked through the door.'

Seven hours away by road. Not to Cole's liking.

'Sorry to bail, but I have to work tomorrow,' she said, into his silence.

'I know the feeling.'

'Your housekeeper doesn't like me.'

'My housekeeper quit. I think the graffiti did her in.'

Silence from Jolie, and then, 'I'm sorry,' she murmured awkwardly. 'I shouldn't have goaded her. Tea-tree oil will get the writing off the tiles. I'm afraid I can't do anything about my surname or the horror your housekeeper felt when she saw me. I did warn you.'

'I heard you the first time. And the second. Just stop with the warnings, Red. I don't need another. The next time you come here I'll have a housekeeper who knows her place.'

More silence at that, and he wished he could see her face and read her thoughts.

'Ophelia-Anne's niece is looking for part-time work,' said Jolie at last. 'She helps us out at the bar when it's busy. Good worker.'

'How old.'

'Oh…twenty? Maybe.'

'The gossip mongers will have me bedding her.'

'Do you care?'

'Will she?'

'You could always interview her and find out.'

Cole took a pull on his beer and padded, still naked, back to the bathroom to stare at Jolie's list. 'What did you want the pen and paper for?'

'I was trying to be polite. Let you know I was heading back to Christchurch.'

'You going to run from this, Jolie?'

'You did,' she said quietly. 'I don't know what you want from me, Cole. Something casual? Or private? Or not? Are you still looking to get me out of your system? What?'

'I don't know,' he said, and tried to read his own face in the mirror. 'For all I know you could be out to wreak vengeance on me for the sins of my father. That's how much trust I think there is between us. Exactly none. Whether we can get past that…' the face in the mirror had no answers for him '…I really don't know. All I know is that I want to see you again. It's the one certainty I own.'

'Would you like to visit me in Christchurch some time?' A tentative offer, but heaven help him he grasped it for the giant leap forwards it was.

'When?'

'Was that a yes?'

'Yes. When?'

'This weekend?'

'Yes. Do I sound desperate?'

'Only a little,' she murmured, with a smile in her voice. 'But I like it when you sound desperate, and dazed and aching for more of me. *Something* has to balance out that screaming lack of trust between us.'

'I'm glad you approve.' For the first time today, Cole felt himself relax. 'I need you here, Red. Why aren't you here?'

'Keep talking,' she murmured. 'No, *really*. Feel free to discuss every little thing you might want from me if I *was* there.'

'Next time.' He looked down at his rapidly swelling anatomy and sighed. 'Did you manage to get some sleep this morning?'

'I did, and thank you. Your bed doesn't fall.'

'Neither will yours, although call me if it starts to. Where do you live? I can be there late Friday night.'

'Do you have a pen and paper handy?'

'No, I have white tiles and a permanent marker.'

She gave him her address. 'Will you fly or drive?'

'Fly.'

'I don't have a car, otherwise I'd offer to pick you up from the airport,' she said, with a note of worry in her voice that brought a frown to his face. 'I live simply, Cole. Don't expect anything grand. You're coming slumming.'

'I'll be there around nine,' he said. 'And just for the record, I'm not coming for the scenery, Jolie. I'm coming for you.'

'I'll endeavour not to disappoint.' With that, she ended the call.

'That's the problem, Red,' he murmured as he set the phone down on the bench. 'You don't.'

Sighing, Cole stepped into the shower, took one look at the writing on the wall, and turned the cold tap on full.

Friday night came and Cole arrived at around nine. He had a slim overnight bag in one hand, a laptop bag in his other, and, as always, he was wearing a suit. He wore them well; Jolie had no complaints. But it spoke of a corporate life she had little knowledge of and responsibilities that went beyond those of a regular man.

Cole seemed to cope well with the pressures of

running Rees Holdings. He'd been raised to lead and from what Jolie could see he did it responsibly and successfully. Whether he ever stopped to notice the little things that went with the passing of a day was anyone's guess.

Jolie, on the other hand, spent a lot of time enjoying the little things that made up the day. The stillness and the silences. The dreaming and the breathing deep. There was a lot of contemplation of soul and of spirit in Jolie's world. A lot of refilling of the creative well. It probably wasn't going to look like work to Cole.

Cole, who up on that fractured mountainside had said scathingly of Jolie Tanner, *'Apparently she fancies herself as an artist.'*

'Come in,' she said nervously, and opened the door to a whole lot of potential hurt. *Come in and examine my life and the way I choose to live it.* It wasn't an invitation she handed out often.

The apartment was a rental, but still hers in so far as everything in it belonged to Jolie. Parts of her world were quite beautiful if a person knew where to look and how to see.

She had wine open on the table. A light supper simmering on the stove. Seafood paella—one of Ophelia-Anne's recipes. She hoped he was hungry.

She'd changed outfits three times already, finally settling on worn jeans and a black long-sleeved, scoop-necked top. She'd tied her hair back in a ponytail with a rainbow striped silk scarf. Not haute couture but not bargain bin, either.

What would he see?

'Come in,' she said again as he stood there just staring at her, and then he was in and the door was closed and his bags were on the ground. He still hadn't said a word.

'I'm not sure how this visiting a woman for the week-end caper works,' he murmured finally. 'I've never done it before. Tell me if I'm doing something wrong.'

The next thing Jolie knew, she was in his arms, sliding into his kiss, and he was feasting on her, savouring her, making her feel like the most important person in his world.

So much for not being able to pick up where they'd left off.

'There's wine,' she said breathlessly when at last he lifted his mouth from hers. 'Rachel picked it and she knows her wines. It's good, even if it's not that expensive.'

'There's you,' he muttered. 'It's really no contest.'

But he sat at her table while she took the paella off the heat and poured him some wine, and his body relaxed some, even if his gaze didn't stray far from her face.

'One of yours?' he asked of an anime cover gracing her fridge door.

'Yes.' One of her first and still one of her finest.

'It's good.'

'It holds a special place in my heart. It got me my job. Your father didn't get me my job, by the way. I asked.'

'Jolie, can we just—'

'Drop it? Yes. I'm already sorry I went there. I don't know why I went there when I so badly want you *here* and seeing what you'll see.' Jolie took a deep breath. 'Let's try that again. Yes, she's called Junkyard Angel and she's one of my favourites. Do you like her?'

'I do.' Cole studied the drawing with gratifying thoroughness. 'She has a look about her. Fragility and worldliness. Caution and strength. She reminds me of you.'

'There's part of me in her, I think. From the heart straight to the paper. Those ones always turn out the best.' Jolie took a quick sip of her wine. Her turn to relax and open up just that little bit more. 'My boss currently has me drawing battle-ready Norse gods. They're not my strength. I'm trying to fix that.'

'How?'

'Would you believe by spending a lot of time lately playing online war games?' Cole didn't laugh and he didn't make any smart comments about that hardly being work, so Jolie continued. 'Most mythical creatures exist within a cultural context that we've built for them over decades, centuries, or even millennia. The trick is to pay homage to a beastie's historical and cultural characteristics while still rendering him fresh and relevant to the current story. And then there's the real trick—bringing something of yourself to the page and making the picture come alive.'

'What characteristics do Norse gods have to have?'

'Horns. Hair. Chests. Weapons. Mythology has them being of fire and ice. The avalanche has given me a whole new respect for ice. I'm good with the terrors of the ice.' Jolie shuddered. 'It's the fire in them that I haven't quite found yet. And a face. I'm having hell's own trouble finding the right face.' She looked at him, head to one side, and teased him, just a little. 'Maybe I'll use yours.'

'Maybe I'll let you.' There was a smile in his eyes now, and a relaxed look about him that hadn't been there earlier.

'So what do you think of the place?' she said

carelessly, as if she didn't much care either way. 'I did tell you it wasn't much, but I pay for it myself. The rent is market rate. Your father doesn't own the apartment. I checked that out too.'

'So did I,' he murmured. 'I'm sorry for the accusations I made on the mountain about what my father had done for you. They weren't correct. I can see that you're making your own way in life, Jolie. I admire that about you. It takes courage. Determination. Belief. But then, I'd already seen those qualities in you on the mountain. I'm beginning to see you clearly, Jolie. I'm starting to trust what I see. You need to stop worrying that I won't.'

Things progressed much easier after that.

Ophelia-Anne's paella recipe did not disappoint, and the wine was good, and as for the company… The company was superb.

Cole helped her clear the meal away from the little wooden table once they'd finished. Jolie's surprise must have shown on her face, because he laughed, and then called her on it too.

'You have a very strange picture of what my life is like,' he told her. 'Yes, I have—or had—a housekeeper. Doesn't mean I've never lifted a plate or filled a dishwasher.'

'Yes, but have you ever *been* a dishwasher?'

'When I was thirteen. I wanted my father to give me a job so he did. I was dishwasher boy at one of our hotels. I learned Rees Holdings from the ground up, Jolie. I've been learning it for sixteen years and I've *always* pulled my own weight and more. Don't think I've been hothoused, I haven't.'

'I believe you,' she said. 'I didn't mean to imply that

you don't know how to work, Cole. I just— You're a man who has everything. I still can't quite figure out what you're doing here. I look at you in your elegant suit and I think of the work responsibilities you shoulder and I'm not sure you're in the right place.'

'It's just a suit,' he said quietly. 'You need to look closer too, Jolie, if you want to see the real me.' He trapped her between the sink and his embrace. 'Can you do that for me?'

'Yes,' she murmured. 'Yes.'

Cole closed his eyes and rested his forehead against hers and for a moment he felt at peace. Was this what his father had felt in Rachel Tanner's arms? This feeling of coming home? Little wonder he'd never been able to give her up. 'Make love with me, Jolie. Please,' he asked her gruffly, and Jolie sighed and kissed him softly on the lips before drawing away. She took his hand and led him to a tiny room dominated by a big, old four-poster bed.

More drawings had been taped around the bedroom's walls. Drawings that overlapped each other and vied for attention, some of them black and white and others in colour, all of them superb. This was Jolie's medium. This was her art.

She saw him looking. How could she not?

'This is what I do,' she said, and vulnerability was back in her eyes. 'These are all the characters I've worked on so far this year. This is my job and my passion. The picture on the fridge was just a preview.'

'They're stunning.' Cole looked closer. 'I'm sorry I ever denigrated your commitment to your art, Jolie. You're insanely gifted.'

'I work hard to stay that way.'

'I see that.'

'You're overdressed,' she said next.

'I can rectify that.' His jacket went, and then his shirt. Jolie came closer and wound her hands in his hair and drew his head down for a kiss. She traced the bow of his upper lip with her tongue and a shudder ripped through him.

'I want to draw you naked,' she said. 'After I have you, I want to draw you.'

'Can I have wings?'

'Maybe,' she murmured, and then ate away all thought of wings with an open-mouthed kiss. 'Maybe I'll give you wings *and* horns.'

He tugged her shirt up over her head, followed her down onto the bed and set about earning both.

Jolie sketched Cole the following morning as he lay there asleep in her bed. The furrow of his spine and the hills and valleys of his shoulders. The skewed line of the pillow and the mop of his hair. Everything about him utterly masculine and so very beautiful. No wings required for the picture to be pure fantasy. Only it wasn't pure fantasy; there'd been no reality bending at all.

When Fantasy Met Reality, she could call it. First time for everything.

Jolie had never understood her mother's willingness to become a married man's mistress. Nothing public, always private. Forever feeding on the crumbs of James Rees's time. All the grief that had gone with it, and for *what*? A lover's *touch*? Why couldn't her mother have been satisfied with some *other* lover's touch? This was the question Jolie had always asked herself.

Finally, she had an answer.

Finally, she knew exactly how lust and longing could capture a person and make reality blur, leaving only the moment. One perfect moment of unity and belonging and to hell and back with the rest of the world and the pain such a moment caused others.

At last, Jolie understood her mother's choices.

And then Cole rolled over onto his back and said, 'Come here,' and she went to him, and straddled him, and stole just one more moment of utter certainty.

She had a vest top and tiny panties on. Just like another reality, another place, and just like then Cole lay on his back and stared up at her and his eyes turned black with intent and his breathing grew ragged.

'Kiss me,' he murmured as his hands went to her head and he drew her down into a kiss so perfect she wanted to weep.

'Touch me,' he said next. As she pushed her panties to one side and positioned herself for his entry and he slid deep inside her and made her complete.

'See me,' she thought she heard him whisper. As he moved deep inside her and made her soar.

CHAPTER EIGHT

COLE visited Jolie again the following weekend, and the one after that, and the one after that. A month passed, and every weekend had Cole in it, and sometimes he flew in on the Friday night and sometimes he came in on the Saturday and on Sunday evening he would leave. One month of glorious privacy and learning to see each other clearly, and the only gossip that Jolie encountered was from her elderly neighbour who'd taken to asking after Jolie's 'young man'.

Life was *very* good.

'What are you doing next weekend?' asked Cole one lazy Sunday afternoon as Jolie stood in the kitchenette mixing pancake batter and smacking the sneaky hand that dipped a finger in it. Cole liked to cook—another revelation that had taken her by surprise, although perhaps it shouldn't have. Cole Rees could turn his hand to anything.

'Not a lot,' she said. 'Why?'

'I'm holding a dinner for Rees Holdings executives and their partners. There'll be a brief speech, plenty of networking. I've made structural changes to various company arms of late. This dinner's mainly about consolidating those changes.'

'So you'll not be coming down, then?' Jolie kept her voice light and hopefully hid her disappointment well.

'No. I'll not be coming down. Doesn't mean I don't want to see you.'

The batter needed to stand. Jolie needed to sit, because she thought she knew what was coming next. The end of the secret fantasy she'd so carefully cultivated. The intrusion of the real world into the fantasy she and Cole had created. Jolie wasn't a fan of the real world.

'So how about it, Jolie?' he murmured. 'You want to come and visit me in Queenstown next weekend? Because I want to take you to that dinner. As my partner.'

'That is such a bad idea.'

'What are you afraid of, Jolie? Gossip?'

'Oh, I think you'll find I'm afraid of plenty more than just gossip.' Jolie set the stirring spoon on the counter and turned troubled eyes on Cole. He stood very still, those green eyes watchful. 'What we have…what we're doing…it works for us here. I don't know how well it's going to work for us in Queenstown.'

'Time to find out, wouldn't you say?'

'Seems a bit…early.'

'Coward,' he said softly.

If the hat fitted… 'I just… What'll your family say? About you and me. About us.'

'Hannah already has her suspicions as to where I go every weekend. She doesn't ask.'

'And you don't say.'

'Like I said,' murmured Cole silkily. 'It's time.'

'What about your mother? Does she have any inkling that you're seeing me?'

'Probably not. We don't talk much.'

'But she *will* be at the dinner.'

'Yes.'

'What say instead of embarking on this whole public dinner snubbing spectacle you be a good son and visit her or call her and tell her about us beforehand?'

'But then she wouldn't be polite.'

Jolie laughed; she couldn't help it. The man had a Machiavellian streak a mile wide. 'You want to force this. Force me on your family and give them no comeback without creating a scene.'

'Yes.' Cole eyed her steadily, every inch the aggressive negotiator who fully intended to get what he wanted. 'You up for it?'

'I honestly don't know.'

'You'll need a gown.'

'I have a gown,' she muttered, with a glare for good measure. 'And before you get cocky, it doesn't sound like a gown event. It sounds like a cocktail-frock event.'

'Do you have one of those?'

'I do. And I still think you're pushing your luck when it comes to forcing me on your family. I doubt they'll be ready. *I'm* not ready. Honestly, Cole,' she said pleadingly. 'Why now? Isn't this working well?'

Cole turned away and paced her tiny living room. She didn't think he saw the pretty in it right now, just the walls, and they were close.

'Yes, it's working well,' he said gruffly. 'Which is why I'm asking you for more. I can't keep leaving my world to come and play in yours, Red. Sometimes I'm going to need you—and want you—in mine. Can't you understand that?'

Jolie stared at him wordlessly. Worriedly. 'Is this a

test? Some kind of experiment to see if this relationship can function in the real world?'

'Yes,' he said curtly, and then, 'No. Goddamn it, why do you have to think of it as a *test*? Why can't you think of it as the next step in our relationship?'

'Why can't you see it for a huge shock to your family?' she retaliated. 'One that needs to be dealt with sensitively rather than rammed down their throats?'

'All right, I'll tell them beforehand,' he snapped. '*Now* will you come out to dinner with me in public?'

'I just think—'

'I know what you think,' he roared. 'You want to treat this relationship like some dirty little secret. I don't. We're doing nothing *wrong. I am not my father, and I am sick to death of wading through the mess he left behind.*'

Cole took a deep breath. Jolie stared at him warily.

'Oh, hell,' he said gruffly. 'I'm sorry, Red. I just have…father issues at the moment. I'm working on it. I will conquer them, but just…answer me this. If your mother had never been my father's mistress, if I was just some lover who'd invited you into his life so you could see if you liked it there, and liked *him* and the way he functioned there, would you come?'

CHAPTER NINE

'YES,' she'd said finally, with two provisos. 'Yes, but you need to tell your family about us beforehand and you need to know that I can be woefully awkward in public. You haven't seen that side of me yet. I cause ripples, and I don't know why, and I never mean to, I just do.'

Deliberate tease. Conscienceless man-eater. Wanton. Wayward. Beautiful. Immoral. No matter what she did or didn't do, Jolie had always attracted the wrong kind of attention. The jealousy of other women. The interest of men. And maybe early on in life she'd blamed James Rees for that fact, but fact was she'd have probably been landed with those name tags anyway. There was a particular type of woman who caused ripples simply by existing. Rachel was one of those.

And so was Jolie.

Her solution had been to stay at home and focus inwards instead of out. 'I'm not all that comfortable in crowds,' she'd told him next. 'I *really* don't socialise much. I'm not very good at it.'

'Jolie, you've worked in a bar half your life. How can a dinner function be too crowded?'

'I have a job to do in the bar and I do it,' Jolie had tried to explain. 'I've practised what to do. I know what not to do. At this dinner I won't have a clue what to do, and I'll have no idea what you want me to be. Can't you see the difference?'

'Just be yourself,' he'd said instantly, as if it were all so very easy. 'Follow my lead when it comes to what to do. I won't abandon you, Red. You have my word.'

And in the end she'd given him hers.

Jolie Tanner had promised to fly to Queenstown on Friday and stay with Cole Rees for the weekend. They'd have dinner together at Rachel's Bar on the Friday night. They'd have dinner with Cole's work colleagues on the Saturday night, and they'd have Sunday to themselves.

Easy.

The week that followed passed a little too quickly for Jolie. Confidence was needed in order to tackle the weekend ahead, and it came in the form of new shoes, and new lipstick. She *almost* lashed out on a gorgeous new dress but in the end sanity and her rapidly diminishing bank balance prevailed. She already had a dress that would be suitable for the occasion, a dress she rarely wore and knew she looked good in. If this weekend turned out okay, then maybe she could think about expanding her wardrobe. If it didn't end well…if she made a complete mess of Cole's world, she'd probably be heading to the nearest art supplies store. Heartache was often accompanied by an outpouring of anguished creativity, or so she'd heard.

Consolation, of a sort.

So many things to be afraid of this coming weekend, but she'd given Cole her word, and on Friday afternoon Jolie finished work at three, headed for the airport and boarded a plane bound for Queenstown.

Cole was not waiting for her as she stepped off the plane. Cole was heading into a meeting and would join her for dinner at the bar at around seven. From there they would head to Cole's house, where Jolie would base herself for the rest of the weekend.

Two nights to fill.

Two dinners to eat.

Two mothers to see.

Jolie hadn't told her mother about Cole yet—not properly. Uncertainty had kept her silent. The need for privacy had stilled her tongue.

And now there was the small matter of not even knowing where to start.

Surely Rachel of all people would understand. Wouldn't she?

The elegant, narrow, hole-in-the-wall bar beckoned to Jolie, as it had always done. Home ground; a place where Jolie knew her role and had built up the appropriate defences against the interest other people took in her. Rachel had helped her with that. Little quips and actions and sayings that Jolie never forgot. Ones that said, *Leave me alone and we'll get on just fine. Don't get too close and I'll smile and everything will be just fine.*

How many *years* had it taken Jolie to feel at home here?

Plenty.

And only her mother knew why. Only her mother and maybe one or two others had ever realised that, beneath Jolie's aloofness or her brazenness or whatever other mask the situation called for, Jolie Tanner was shy.

Really, *really* shy. Almost debilitatingly so.

Jolie's overnight bag went in the corner space behind

the bar when she got in. She slung a black serving apron on, and with it she put on her bar mask, the one that went on easy and stayed in place for hours at a time. She walked up to her mother—who was busy building three Guinnesses—and kissed her on the cheek.

'Be still my beating heart,' said one of the customers. 'There's two of them.'

And Jolie grinned and said, 'Word has it that if you're drunk enough you'll see four.' And the words came out lazy and knowing, and the customer smiled his appreciation as Jolie slipped away, and headed out back to Ophelia-Anne's domain to catch up with the rest of her family and maybe, just maybe, catch up on a little hometown gossip along the way.

Cole had indeed hired Ophelia-Anne's niece as his new housekeeper. Three days a week, nine to three. Odie had been on the job for over a month now.

'He sleeps there and he showers there,' Odie said cheerfully. 'Never messes up the kitchen, never has anyone over. How the hell he got his reputation is beyond me.'

'Maybe he got his the same way Jolie got hers,' murmured Ophelia-Anne, who was busy shucking oysters and arranging them on ice. 'By default.'

'Maybe he used to play hard but doesn't any more,' said Jolie. 'Less time for play. More focus on the work. Cole works hard, that much I do know. He takes his responsibility to the Rees empire seriously.'

'Like James,' said Ophelia-Anne. 'I remember when that wife of his threatened to destroy all he'd worked for if he divorced her. Not take it, because he'd have let her. Destroy it. She'd have done it too.'

'James wanted to divorce his wife?' said Jolie. This was news that had never happened her way before.

'And take up with your mama,' said Ophelia-Anne with a nod. 'But Christina Rees, she knew where to apply the pressure. And then there were the kiddies. They may not have liked their daddy spending time with your mama, but James was there when they needed him and that counts for plenty in my book. He did what he could to make things work for everyone. Your mama misses him. We all do.'

Jolie heard the words. Words that brought with them yet another new spin on what she thought she knew of James Rees's affair with her mother. But it was more current affairs that concerned her. Like the one she'd embarked on with Cole.

The one she wanted to keep secret, but Cole didn't. The one she'd agreed to make public this weekend.

Jolie found her mother in the storeroom stacking cartons. She started helping, no direction required. This was the easy bit. The words she wanted to come next were going to be hard.

'Mama, what's it like for you here now that James is gone?' she asked quietly and Rachel stopped hauling and put her hands to her back and stretched it out, and favoured Jolie with a faint smile.

'The thing is, I never built my life around him,' said Rachel softly. 'Finally that feels like a bonus.'

'But you still miss him.'

'I'll always miss him.' Her mother's gaze had turned quizzical. 'Jolie, where are we going with this?'

'Well…I met a man,' said Jolie. Which seemed as good a place to start as any. 'And I've been getting to know him. And I've asked here tonight so that you can get to know him too, only you already kind of *do* know him, and it's complicated, and I'm scared he's going to make you sad, and I'm pretty sure he's going to remind you of James.' Jolie took a deep breath. 'Mama, it's Cole.'

Rachel said nothing, leaving Jolie only uncertainty to work with.

'He's been visiting me in Christchurch, and that's been working out fine. Great, even, but he wanted me to visit him here this weekend instead. He wants me to go to some Rees work function with him tomorrow night.' Jolie chewed her lip uncertainly. 'I don't know how well that's going to go down but I said I would. I'm worried about not fitting in and how his family's going to react. I'm worried about how *you* feel about me seeing him. I don't know if you know him or like him or whether he reminds you too much of James and you'd rather not have him round. I just thought… I just wanted to bring him here. He wanted… He thought it was time we let people know about us. That we're seeing each other. Properly.'

'I see.' Rachel's smile barely qualified as one but it was a start and Jolie was grateful. 'What is it you want from me, Jolie?'

'Your understanding, mostly.'

'You have it. Love can be complicated. It can sneak up unexpectedly and make fools of us all. I wondered— after the example I set for you—I was afraid you wouldn't ever open up your heart to anyone. I needed to believe that one day you would.'

'Mama, it's *Cole*.'

'Yes, I heard.' Another faint smile.

'Cole, who I've spent a lot of time hating and whose

lifestyle scares me—there's so many important people in it. His mother and sister despise me. I'm really not all that fond of them. And every now and then Cole and me, we trip over you and James and that's *awkward*.'

'And I'm sorry for that, I really am.' But Rachel's eyes had started to smile. 'It's going to be quite a ride.'

'I'm not sure I want this ride.'

'Don't say that,' whispered Rachel. 'Don't you see? This ride you're on—this falling in love—it's the only ride worth taking.'

'But what if I disappoint him? Mama, what if I can't cope? With the people, and the lifestyle Cole leads? What if I can't be what he needs me to be?'

'Then the ride ends,' said Rachel simply. 'And you'll be a little bit sadder, and a whole lot wiser, but you'll have known love, and experienced what people will do in the name of it. Is that really such a bad thing?'

Jolie didn't know. 'I'm not sure he sees me,' she said haltingly. 'I don't think he knows just how little use I'm going to be to him at his work dinners and the like.'

'You learned to handle the social situations that arise in a bar, didn't you?' said her mother. 'You handle yourself beautifully.'

'Mama, it took *years*.'

'What? You don't have a few to spare?' Jolie's mother spared her a smile. 'Maybe it *will* take years before you're comfortable in Cole's world. Maybe it'll take courage, and patience, and understanding on Cole's part. Doesn't mean you won't get there eventually. You always have.'

'I'm scared,' whispered Jolie.

'I know, baby.'

'I don't want to disappoint him. Or me.'

'I know that too.' Rachel drew Jolie into her embrace and Jolie let herself be comforted. 'Believe in yourself, Jolie. Be true to yourself and to the people you love. Love unconditionally and maybe, just maybe, unconditional love will find you. They're the only beliefs I have worth teaching you.'

'I love you,' whispered Jolie.

'And I love you.'

'I've wondered a lot of things about your relationship with James over the years,' murmured Jolie. 'I wondered why you never asked for more of him. I wondered how you could be content with so little of his time. But I've never wondered why he fell in love with you.' Jolie pulled back and sent her mother a wobbly smile. 'How could he not?'

Cole came into the bar at around seven and from the way he was dressed he'd come straight from his office. Business suit and tie, snowy white shirt cuffs and a grim cast to his mouth—all the hallmarks of a wearisome week. But he smiled when he saw her and some of the grimness melted away and charm took its place.

He headed for the quietest slice of bar top available, empty space where the lights were low and the sheen on the polished wooden surface was muted. Jolie finished serving a customer and headed towards him, more than a little nervous now that the moment for meeting him here had arrived.

She had no mask for this. She didn't have her mother's unassailable centre, or confidence, or any kind of experience whatsoever when it came to greeting a lover in public. Not this lover—who'd come to mean so much to her in such a small amount of time.

'Cole Rees. Fancy seeing you here.' Jolie put her elbows on the bar and leaned forward. 'What'll you have?'

'A seat.' Cole eyed her quizzically. 'Maybe a drink. You see, I'm meeting a woman here for dinner—at least, that's what I thought I was doing, although it's possible she's had to go to work. You'd know her if you saw her. Eyes to drown in. A smile that can bring a man to his knees.'

'You're going to have to be a little more specific than that.' He knew how to put her at ease, this man. He knew how to make a woman smile.

'Well,' he drawled. 'She also knows how to put fire into the heart of even the iciest of Norse gods. And she's a tease.' Cole leaned forward too, and the distance between them diminished. The intensity of his regard quadrupled. 'Kiss me.'

'You really want to do this?' Jolie pulled back, just a little. Not sure. Not sure.

'Why? Are you worried about your reputation?'

'Not mine. Yours.'

'Don't be. What else are you worried about, Red?'

'Ruining your plans this weekend. Ruining this for both of us.' There, she'd said it.

'Don't be. Kiss me.'

'Autocrat.'

'I'm getting there,' murmured Cole. 'Which is why I need you, for balance. Kiss me, Jolie. Please.'

So Jolie leaned in again and pressed her lips to his. One kiss, light and easy. And still he swept her away to a place where nothing else mattered and no anchor could be found.

'There,' he said finally, once he'd pulled away. 'Was that so hard?'

'No.' But she glanced warily around the bar, looking for ripples and whispers and finding them.

'Now say it with a little more certainty,' he commanded softly. 'And then sit and have dinner with me. If tongues want to wag, let them.'

'Always orders with you. Why is that?' she said, but she drew Cole a beer, and poured a Semillon Blanc for herself. She told him the specials of the day and when he asked her what was good she put an order in to Ophelia-Anne for two seafood specials, and then she slipped off her black bartending apron and headed around the other side of the bar to join him.

Just Jolie Tanner and the lover who was well on his way to stealing her heart.

'How did your latest set of drawings shape up?' he asked her as they took their drinks over to an empty booth. She'd been wrestling with the Angel Gabriel through the week. She'd mentioned him to Cole on the phone. They would have talked about him if they'd been in her little apartment, and it settled Jolie, as small talk often did.

'They got the nod. My thanks to your thighs, your chest, and possibly your face. The wings were just icing on the cake as far as I was concerned. I'm now drawing scary vampire lords for a different project. Maybe I can give them your hands.'

Cole had nice hands. Large but lean. Slow.

'What's the project?' he asked.

'Television series episode. I get to deliver up the monster of the week.' She said this with relish, because it was relish she felt.

'Jolie Tanner loves her work,' he murmured, leaning back against the padded back of the booth and lifting his beer to his lips.

'Yes, she does.' Jolie smiled. 'How's *your* work going?'

'It has its moments. And its surprises. I got a stack of paperwork in from Rees legal this morning. You're giving back the real estate my father left you.'

'Yes.' Jolie's wariness returned in spades. Not a comfortable topic for them, this one, for all that they'd come a long way.

'Why?'

'I didn't want it.'

'It would have set you up well, Jolie. Got you out of the rental market.'

'I know.' A tiny negative shake of her head. 'Let's just say I still have a few too many unresolved feelings about some of your father's decisions and the way he chose to live his life to be accepting his gifts. I just don't want them.'

'Bitter,' said Cole.

'A little. Okay, a lot. I just wish...that he'd been stronger somehow. That he'd made a decision one way or another. That he hadn't tried to have it all and hurt so many people in the process.'

'I know the feeling.'

'That bitterness doesn't extend to you.'

Cole's lips twisted into the semblance of a smile. 'I know that feeling too.'

'So tell me again what this work dinner of yours is supposed to achieve?' she said next, for they'd grown adept at skating over the mess their elders had made.

'Cohesion, mostly. A stronger focus on the future.

Silverlake was underinsured. We've gone way over budget on another of our projects. And people are starting to get nervous about some of the structural changes I'm planning to make to Rees Holdings.'

'You want to sell the master plan.'

'Exactly.'

'Am I supposed to *help* you sell the master plan?' Jolie's apprehension kicked and kicked hard. 'Because you know I'm not going to be of any help to you in that regard, right? And if you're hoping that bringing me along is going to show you as being in a comfortable and settled relationship, I'm not sure I'm going to be much help with that, either.'

'So, are you saying we're *not* in a comfortable and settled relationship? I don't know, Red.' Cole's smile came slow and surprisingly sweet. 'I'm feeling pretty good in that regard.'

'Cole—

'Just be there,' he interrupted quietly. 'That's all I'm asking. Just be there with me.'

It seemed such a little thing to ask.

The food came quickly—Ophelia-Anne must have bumped them to the top of her list. Cole devoured his and half of her very generous serving too. Jolie watched him with a wry smile. Ophelia-Anne's cooking tended to have that effect on people, unless you were used to it, at which point restraint became slightly more achievable.

She watched him trade banter with Odie when Odie came to clear their plates. He defended the pitiful emptiness of his fridge and then accepted with alacrity Odie's offer to make grocery shopping for him part of her housekeeping routine.

'Leave me a list,' said Odie cheerfully. 'I'll shop for you on Mondays and Fridays. Are you ready for the dessert menu now?'

They decided against dessert.

'Coffee's good here,' said Odie encouragingly, and Jolie nodded her agreement. They couldn't leave yet. There was something they needed to do here first.

'Odie, would you ask my mother if she'd like to join us for coffee?' asked Jolie, for her mother had kept her distance from the moment Cole had come in, and that wasn't part of anyone's plan.

At least she didn't *think* it was part of anyone's plan.

'About that bitterness,' she said cautiously. 'We're trying not to let it extend to the living, right? You're still okay about meeting my mother?'

'I'm ready,' he said with a crooked smile. 'Relax, Jolie. It's going to be fine.'

When Rachel came over with coffee for three, Cole stood while she set the coffee down, and then he pulled out a chair for her and kept right on standing until she'd taken a seat.

Jolie smiled and sat on her hands to quell her nervousness. 'Cole, this is my mother, Rachel. Mama, this is Cole.'

And Rachel smiled and said, 'I've seen manners like that before.'

And Cole said, 'I learned them at my not-so-sainted father's knee,' and his delivery was so droll that Rachel laughed, and Jolie realised that he *had* been ready for this meeting, and that he was determined, above all, to leave the past behind and move on.

They could do this.

They *were* doing this.

Rachel liked Cole's approach. Rachel slipped easily into conversation about plans to reopen Silverlake.

One mother down.

One more to go.

Cole and Jolie left the bar with six raspberry friands, half a chocolate mudcake and a bottle of very nice champagne. Cole's smile had turned wry when he'd spotted the champagne, but he thanked Rachel nicely for the goodies, and when they got outside into the crisp snowy air he asked Jolie no questions about another bottle of champagne in another place and time so she told him no lies.

'The champagne reminded me of something,' he murmured.

'It did?' she murmured non-committally. Maybe she'd been a little hasty with her thinking that Cole was going to let the similarity between this bottle of champagne and another one just like it pass him by.

'It did. One of the clean-up teams at Silverlake re-covered the contents of your box the other day. Most of it went in the bin but I had them take the bedspread to the dry-cleaner's. It's at my place. You might want to give it back to your mother at some stage.'

'So…you know what was in the box.'

'Your mother's things from my father's cabin,' he said. 'Am I right?'

'Yes.'

'Don't sweat it, Jolie,' he offered quietly. 'I'm not. It's in the past. I am strongly focused on overcoming the past and forging a future these days. One with you in it.'

'Did you tell Hannah and your mother about us?' asked Jolie.

'Not yet.' And as Jolie's eyes widened, 'But I will.'

'*When?*' Jolie tried to stem her rising panic. 'Cole, you gave me your *word*.'

'In the morning. Before the dinner. Trust me.'

'I don't think you realise how important it is that you give people space with this, not back them into a corner. Hannah hasn't spoken to me since I was *twelve*. Your mother's going to feel betrayed. Again. Couldn't you have given them a little more time to get *used* to the idea of you and me together?'

'They'll get used to it.'

He didn't see, thought Jolie, biting her lip. He didn't want to see. 'I think the extent of your family's opposition to me is going to surprise you, Cole.'

'*Nothing* my family does surprises me, Red. When it gets too ridiculous I simply ignore them.'

'Really?'

'Really. We Reeses are exceptionally good at ignoring the things we don't want to see,' he said, and he gave her that sinner's smile and she shook her head and got in his car. 'Little survival mechanism of ours.'

'Just so long as you realise that my survival mechanism is retreat,' muttered Jolie darkly. 'This is going to be a disaster.'

'No, it's not. You're forgetting something,' he said.

'What?'

'You and me.'

Cole's house was still as impressive as ever. They made it to the kitchen this time. Presumably the idea was to have some dessert.

And then dessert was forgotten as Cole lifted her onto

the counter and began an assault on her mouth that had nothing to do with retreat and everything to do with pent-up, clawing need.

Jolie knew that sex was not enough to base a relationship on. They still had to like each other and respect each other and fit as a couple into the world around them. But right now, with Cole undoing her coat buttons and Jolie threading her hands through his hair, it seemed that sex for pleasure's sake…intense, mind-stealing, body-bending sex…was surely enough to be going on with.

Morning came and Jolie slept. Cole got up and headed for the shower and after that the kitchen. Decent coffee. One of last night's sweets to eat while he pondered the question of exactly what he wanted from Jolie Tanner.

He'd stripped their encounters of the element of the forbidden, hoping it might lessen his craving for her.

It hadn't.

He'd gorged himself on her, thinking that the novelty would surely wear off and his interest in her would wane.

It hadn't.

He'd waited for *her* to find fault with *him*. To take a deeper look at the things he could never give her. Like a fresh start with a lover whose family didn't give a damn that Jolie's mother had been mistress to a married man. He'd waited for Jolie to pull back and put a stop to this… whatever it was.

She hadn't.

So here he was, wondering what she wanted for breakfast and hoping like hell this weekend went the way he wanted it to go, which was smoothly. Jolie would fit into his world with ease and that would be one anxiety of hers gone. Hannah and Christina would be civil, if not exactly welcoming, and that would be another barrier gone. And then they could get on with the business of arranging their lives so that they saw more of each other. He knew Jolie's work was important to her and that she had no desire to leave her job in Christchurch and return to Queenstown, but surely they could come to some arrangement.

Maybe he could set up an office in Christchurch.

Maybe Jolie could explore opportunities to work more from home. They could split their time between Christchurch and Queenstown. They could compromise.

If this dinner went well…

This dinner had to go well.

Cole was halfway through his first coffee when Hannah's Audi came roaring up his driveway and Hannah emerged from the driver's seat. She had her hair in a ponytail and jeans and a jacket on. Cole hardly recognised her. Hannah was big on looking as if she'd just stepped off the pages of a fashion magazine. Her mother's daughter, through and through.

This Hannah, the one with the ponytail and the bounce in her step, grabbed a folder from her back seat and let herself into his house without knocking—more fool him for giving her a key. She shot him a smile when she saw him in the kitchen.

'I'm so glad you're up,' she said. 'I've been working on it all week, but I think I've finally fixed the budget problem on the Shore Hotel project. We're going for tiered levels of accommodation rather than outright luxury. We're starting low end. As the hotel starts to turn a profit, we can upgrade, level by level. I think it'll work.'

'Hannah—'

'Derek thinks it'll work, but I need you to look at it now so we can tell people it's all fixed at Monday's board meeting. And can I have a coffee? I'd kill for a coffee. I stayed up half the night running the new figures.'

Cole shook his head and headed for the coffee pot. Hannah ran red-hot or Hannah ran cold—there was no middle ground with her. 'I'll take a look.'

Cole set a steaming black coffee down in front of his sister and pushed Ophelia-Anne's cake box towards her too. Hannah watched her food-versus-exercise ratios with the rabid intensity of a zealot, but she had a weakness for sweet things and Cole enjoyed watching her succumb to temptation on occasion. 'Are you planning on staying for breakfast?' he said next. 'Because if you are, you should probably know that I have company. She's asleep at the moment but when she gets up we're going to have breakfast. You're welcome to join us. It'd mean a lot to me if you did. I think…it'd mean a lot to her too.'

Hannah paused with a little raspberry topped cake halfway to her lips. She set it down on the counter gently. She brushed the remaining crumbs from her hands.

'Jolie Tanner,' she said flatly. 'You brought Jolie Tanner *here*.' Hannah wasn't psychic. She was just uncannily good at connecting people's dots.

'This is my house,' he said evenly. 'Where else would I take her?'

'Oh, let me see… A Motel 6? Some dingy little out-of-the-way cabin in the mountains? You seem hell-bent on following in our father's footsteps. It'd be a shame not to go all the way.'

'I am *nothing* like our father, Hannah, and you know it. I have no wife, no children and every right to bring whoever I want here. I'm not *doing* this for kicks. I want Jolie Tanner in my life. Chances are I'm hell deep in love with her.'

'How can you be in love with her? You hardly even *know* her.'

'I've been seeing her since the avalanche, Han. And I'm loving what I see.'

'No.' Hannah shook her head. 'Cole, no. How can you *do* this? To our mother? To *me*?'

'Do what? Fall for a woman I have every right to fall for? What happened between Jolie's mother and our father wasn't Jolie's fault. It has *nothing* to do with us.'

'Cole, you *can't.*'

'Why not? Jolie's not her *goddamn mother. I am not my father.*' Too loud, his voice now, and he tried to tamp it down, heaven help him, he did. 'How long do we have to wear other people's mistakes, Hannah? Answer me that?'

'You don't understand. I want to move on, I *do*. But I can't even look at Jolie without seeing Rachel and remembering what she did to our family. As for our mother…how do you think *she'll* feel about inviting Jolie into our lives? Dredging up all those old hurts that she's only just buried. She is *never* going to acknowledge Jolie Tanner as a suitable partner for you. How can you not know this?'

'Maybe—'

'No, Cole! There is no *maybe*. What's more, if you

choose Jolie over family, Christina's going to take all those years' worth of humiliation and betrayal out on *you*. She'll crack. She'll ruin Rees Holdings, just like she always threatened to do, only this time she'll *do* it because Daddy won't be there to stop her.'

'You going to help her, Hannah? Because she's going to need the majority vote to do it and I'm sure as hell not giving her mine.'

'Cole, please!' It was the cry of a bewildered child and it tore at Cole's heart. 'Don't do this. Don't make me choose between the brother I love and a mother who'll be left with no one if I desert her too.'

'It doesn't have to be like that,' Cole said raggedly. 'If you would both just see reason—'

'Oh, Cole, grow up! Reason's got *nothing* to do with this.' Hannah's tears were in full flow now; there'd be no stopping them. 'You're breaking my heart.'

'You're breaking mine too, Han.'

'Please, Cole. You'll find someone else eventually. Someone everyone can love and accept. You *will*. Just give up Jolie Tanner.'

But Cole just shook his head. 'Can't do it, Han. Won't. Jolie's coming to the dinner with me tonight. Get used to seeing her at my side because that's where she's going to be. As for Christina taking it in her head to get at me by ruining Rees Holdings—that company is mine to make thrive, not hers to destroy. I'll fight her if I have to. I'll fight her with everything I've got.'

Hannah shot him a tear-drenched glance on her way to the door. Guess she wasn't staying for breakfast after all. 'You're going to have to.'

Cole dropped his head and closed his eyes as Hannah's shiny Audi tore down the driveway with Hannah in it.

He ran his hand through his hair and opened his eyes again, his gaze heading left at the sound of movement. He almost groaned then because Jolie was up. Jolie, leaning against the doorway to the lounge room, wearing his shirt, with her hair all mussed and her feet bare, watching him with those all-seeing grey eyes. 'How much did you hear?' he asked gruffly.

'All of it.'

'Right.' How to bare a soul and expose the fractures in a family all in one fell swoop. 'Right.'

'Do you want to talk about it?' asked Jolie quietly.

'I just did.'

'Do you want me to leave?'

'No.'

'It might be better if I did.'

'For who? For my mother and Hannah?'

'For you.'

'No.' He ran his hand through his hair again. 'Look, can you just forget you ever heard that particular conversation?'

'No.' Jolie's gaze was clear, and faintly cool. No lover's teasing glance or easy words. 'There are parts of it I want to remember. I quite liked the "chances are I'm hell deep in love with her" bit. Nice word choice, Romeo.'

'Jolie, I—'

'And I quite liked the bit where you refused to give me up. Even in the face of all manner of wrath raining down on you. Of course, it probably has more to do with you resenting being told what to do than it does with you being hell deep in love with me, but still…'

'Why is it,' he muttered, 'that women are forever asking a man if he wants to talk about something and then, when he says no, they go ahead and analyse a situation to death anyway?'

Jolie had found her way to the counter. She leaned in beside him. Plucked a friand from the box and eyed the steaming coffee he'd set out for Hannah. 'You don't mind if I drink Hannah's coffee, do you?' she asked sweetly. 'I noticed she never got around to it and it seems a shame to waste it.'

'Milk's in the fridge,' he said warily, and watched as Jolie retrieved it and fussed over the little things like putting the teaspoon in the dishwasher and putting away the milk, while he stewed and he seethed and his temper ratcheted up a notch. A declaration of love and devotion from *her* side wouldn't have gone astray, but he didn't get one. Maybe he'd misjudged her. The strength of their relationship. The joy that came of being together. Maybe he saw only what he wanted to see. 'Talk to me, Jolie.'

'All right,' she said finally. 'For better or for worse— and I'm predicting worse—I'll come to your dinner and I'll stand at your side. I'm not as certain as you are that I can fit in your world or be a part of it that doesn't hold you back. Sometimes I get shy. Really, really shy. Sometimes I don't mix well at all and all I want to do is run screaming to the safety of my drawings and my imagination, where I'm the one in control and can make things exactly the way I want them to be.'

'I can support you,' he said, his gaze sharp. 'At dinner tonight, I *will* support you.'

'I know you will.' Jolie smiled faintly. 'I know your strength of mind, Cole. I've seen it firsthand. But you lied, you know. About ignoring your family. Pretending that you didn't care either way whether you had their support or not when it came to you choosing to be with me. You do care. You care a lot. About Hannah. About your stewardship of Rees Holdings. I still haven't figured out your feelings for your mother.'

'Neither have I,' he muttered.

'Do you usually get on with your mother?'

'Next question, Red.'

'So, you don't.'

'My mother is not an open person,' he said finally. 'I find it hard to tell where she's coming from. Or where she's going, for that matter. I've never had the knack.'

'Does Hannah have the knack?' asked Jolie, and Cole shrugged.

'She and Hannah are close,' he said. 'My mother's in the habit of using Hannah to shore up her own position. Hannah can't see it.'

'Happy families,' said Jolie.

'Not so much.' Cole had had enough of this particular conversation. He wanted the troubled look gone from Jolie's big grey eyes. 'Trust me,' he murmured, putting his hand to her face. 'Don't bail on me now.'

'You're asking a lot, Cole. You're asking so much from everyone in pushing for this meeting. Hannah. Your mother. Me. What happens when we let you down?'

'You haven't yet.'

'That doesn't mean I won't. Sometimes I feel like you're deliberately forcing this meeting, Cole, because deep down inside you want this relationship to fail.'

'You're wrong.'

'I hope so.' If anything, Jolie looked even more troubled. 'Because there are easier ways to end a relationship. Less destructive ways.'

'And I know them all,' he said quietly. 'For the last time, Jolie. I don't want you to go.'

Jolie dressed for dinner with care. Not all women could wear the colour gold, but Jolie could and it was the colour of her dress. Muted, not shiny, an old-gold silk sheath that finished at her knees and put her in mind of Holly Golightly's little black dress in *Breakfast At Tiffany's*. It was simple. It was stunning. And with her hair up in a princess bun, and her grandmother's pearls clasped around her neck and dangling from her ears and the rest of her toilette complete, Jolie felt ready for just about anything Cole's family and his colleagues could throw at her. She picked up her coat and slung it over her arm. Vintage Chanel, in deepest black velvet. Like the pearls, it had belonged to her grandmother, and like the pearls it bestowed elegance and status upon its wearer.

They could fault her for many things tonight, and probably would. Inappropriate attire would not be one of them.

Cole was not in the bedroom. Men like Cole had it easy when it came to dressing to impress. A tailor-made black dinner suit, a brush of his teeth, a fresh shave and a comb through his hair. It had taken him all of five minutes. The world was unjust.

Mind you, he'd spent the better part of the afternoon going over the figures Hannah had left him along with taking phone calls and making them. Jolie had let him be, unpacked her sketchbook and taken herself out into Cole's garden. Gnomes and faeries played well in nature's wild hollows and there were plenty of those hollows to be found around here. Besides, she'd needed the break. A little break from reality.

He'd called her in at five; it was now almost six. He didn't look nervous. 'Do *I* look nervous?' she asked him aloud.

'No,' he said.

'Oh, good.' Hard to believe, but good.

'You look stunning, Jolie.'

'Thank you.' The look in Cole's eyes gave her confidence. Allowed her to smile and mean it. 'Shall we go?'

'I think we should,' he said huskily. 'Otherwise we're not going to get there at all.'

The evening started well enough. Drinks in the bar of the fancy hotel where some of Cole's managers were staying. Later they would move on to the hotel restaurant, but for now it was the meet and greet, with Cole making the introductions and Jolie doing her best to remember names. That everyone seemed to know each other didn't help. That half of them wanted to talk business with Cole didn't help, either.

What was a corporate-wife type supposed to do when that happened? Drift away? Have an opinion on the matter? She knew precious little about Rees Holdings other than it seemed to encompass a great many individual businesses, with precious little rhyme or reason as to why. Cole, it seemed, was in the process of centralising the business processes that were common to them all. It sounded smart but some people had reservations. Most of those who did have reservations were older men, James's age, with their own definite ideas on how things should be done.

The phrases 'James would have…' and 'Your father would have…' prefaced so many of their arguments.

Just how sick of that particular comparison was Cole?

Just how hard was he having to fight to get out from under the shadow of his father? Cole hated being compared to James, that much she did know. And yet Cole was more like his father than he realised. Persuasive. Insistent. And just that little bit uncaring of the effect his action in bringing her here tonight was having on others in the same way that James had cared little for how his adultery had affected those closest to him. It spoke of either great passion or emotional selfishness.

Or both.

Jolie wasn't entirely comfortable with either.

'I'll just be mingling,' she murmured, when the grey-haired gentleman who'd been talking to Cole eventually paused for breath. Mingling, as if it were the easiest thing in the world to do.

Cole shot her a sharp glance and looked around. 'Dinner won't be too far off. We're only waiting on a couple more people.'

Jolie scanned the compact crowd too. No Hannah. No Christina Rees, either. Cole had phoned Christina that morning. He'd told her he was taking Jolie to the dinner. Maybe Christina Rees had decided to boycott the event altogether.

Jolie's predominant emotion was one of relief.

Pinning on a confident smile, Jolie stepped away from Cole's protection, a little foray of her own in a room full of strangers. This was what she'd promised herself she would do. Pick a mask, any mask, and give fitting in here her best shot.

The people nearest to her were a group of corporate wives in perhaps their mid-fifties. Four of them altogether, chatting amiably. She caught their eye, started towards them, and watched them smoothly drift away.

She tried another trio of women. These ones were younger, less experienced in the game of social put-down. They managed a few comments on the weather before one of them noticed her husband beckoning, and another one discovered she'd lost her handbag and both she and her friend went off to find it, leaving Jolie standing there in a circle of one.

And then Hannah arrived on the arm of a steely-eyed, granite-faced man and everything got infinitely worse.

The man headed for Cole's side. Hannah headed for the nearest group of women, the older ones, who had this game down pat. They greeted her like a daughter and Hannah Rees let them.

Jolie headed for the bar—not to drink, just to be there. A half-familiar place, and a barman who chatted and flirted and made the place feel inviting, as all good barmen should. But the drink she wanted was a soda water and was all too soon made, and the barman went on to serve another customer.

Squaring her shoulders, Jolie turned around and surveyed Cole's colleagues and their partners once more, looking for a way in. One stylish but heavily pregnant woman in her thirties was sitting by herself and people-watching with interest, but Jolie didn't approach her. The woman looked as if she needed the rest and she wouldn't get that if the minute Jolie sat down beside her she felt compelled to get up and walk away.

Jolie approached a duo of men instead, deliberately

chosen because they were in their late thirties or early forties and they hadn't brought partners with them. Women got defensive when Jolie approached their man. Some of them got downright hostile. Always had.

The two men were welcoming. They likcd what they saw. One was more polite than the other. Less inclined to stand there and stare at her face.

'You're here with…who again?' asked the polite one.

'Cole.'

The man nodded. He had smiley eyes and absolutely no sexual interest in Jolie at all. Maybe he'd asked the question for his friend's benefit. His friend who very quickly remembered his manners.

The conversation flowed freely enough. They asked her what she did for a living and she told them. They talked about Tolkien and movies, rangers and orcs. Jolie hadn't been a part of the Rings caravan, but she'd benefited immensely from the booming special effects industry it had left behind. Another man joined them, this one a Warhammer fan who still collected and painted figurines. Watching what the Warhammer artists came up with next was one of Jolie's favourite pastimes. Two more men joined them and talk of Warhammer turned to talk of online gaming. Battle strategy wasn't a passion of Jolie's but she knew her way around the various gaming platforms. The artwork there was cutting edge too.

Eventually, Jolie fell silent and let others carry the conversation. She didn't have to be the centre of attention in a circle full of men. She didn't *want* to be the centre of attention in a circle full of men. She just needed a group to stand with, a group of people who wouldn't take one look at her and walk away.

She sipped her soda and glanced around to see where Cole was.

Over near the doorway, with his back turned towards her, deep in conversation with Hannah and the steely-eyed man.

She wished another woman would come and join the group she was in, but not one of them did.

They just watched her with varying degrees of hostile glee.

'Look at her,' they'd be saying. 'Surrounded by men. Flirting with them. Encouraging them. Can't he *see* what she is?' While knowing all along that they had channelled her towards the men in the first place.

Time flowed on.

Cole seemed to have disappeared.

Jolie excused herself from the conversation and took her now-empty soda glass back to the barman. She asked him where the restrooms were.

Out the door, round to your right.

Fair enough.

'Probably fake,' said one woman, touching her hands to her pearls as Jolie passed by.

'Probably a cow,' said Jolie, and with a dismissive glance kept right on walking.

Jolie stepped out of the room and found Cole just about to step in. 'We're moving in to dinner,' he said, when he saw her. 'Couple of seating changes that needed dealing with.'

'Your mother's not coming,' said Jolie. 'Who else didn't come?'

'No one. You're doing fine, Red. Thanks for giving me the space to talk business with people. Appreciated.'

Jolie favoured him with a wry smile, her bartending smile, full of a confidence she was far from feeling. 'You're welcome. Half your regional managers are online gamers. We found common ground.'

'Just so long as when you finish reducing them to willing slaves you come and find me.' Cole leaned in and kissed her then, not fleetingly, but a promise of things to come.

'Go,' she said, before she drew him into a dark and private corner and kept him there. 'Go do business.'

She headed for the restroom. The narrow hallway that led to them had not been empty. One of Cole's division managers—an older gent—was coming towards her, smiling genially. '"But, soft! What light through yonder window breaks?"' he said. 'You must be Cole's young lady.' He stopped before her and extended his hand. 'Rufus Edwards.'

Rufus Edwards had clammy hands.

He was also one of those people in favour of capturing her hand with *both* of his.

'Of course, I knew your mother too, so I recognised you at once,' said Rufus smoothly. 'Beautiful woman, your mother. Exquisite. Such a pity James wasn't one to share.'

Jolie wanted her hand back.

'I think you'll find, though, that young Cole has a far shorter attention span than his father had,' the man continued affably. 'Young people these days have no staying power.'

'I'd like my hand back, please, Mr Edwards,' said Jolie through gritted teeth. 'Now.'

Rufus's smile widened, but he did as he was bid. 'If I may just point out,' he murmured, 'that's really no way to speak to a potential client.'

'You're not a potential client, old man. You couldn't afford me. And tell me…' Jolie leaned in confidentially '…which one back there is your wife? I'd so love to meet her.'

Rufus departed.

Jolie found the restroom and headed straight for the basin. Soap, she needed soap to coat her hands with. Soap to wash away the unpleasantness of Rufus Edwards's touch and the ugliness of his words. Two squirts from the dispenser weren't enough. Jolie added a third as she stared in the large bathroom mirror and examined her face, her looks, and tried to figure out what it was about her that brought out the worst in others.

Her looks? Her manner? A reputation that had always preceded her? *What?*

Cole thought she was holding up just fine in his world. Jolie disagreed.

Hands beneath the water now to get rid of the soap. Then, with her hands to the edge of the porcelain half-basin, Jolie closed her eyes and wished herself back in Christchurch in her shabby little apartment with its dinky view and paper friends all around her. She didn't need these types of people in her life—the kind who tore others down in order to lift themselves up. The kind who behaved without conscience and then hid behind expensive clothes and whopping great lies, confident that their status would protect them, especially against someone who had none. And usually it did.

What was the bet slimy Shakespeare-quoting Rufus was at that moment telling his lemon-mouthed wife that

Jolie had offered him her sexual favours for a price? Covering his backside. Getting even for the slight. *That* was what she was up against here. And she didn't know if she was strong enough to fight against it.

'You can do this,' she whispered aloud, but her voice lacked conviction. 'You promised you'd give it your best shot.'

The sound of a cubicle door opening behind her caused Jolie to snap her eyes open. Her gaze met that of the other woman in the mirror. A woman with glossy black hair styled straight around a face that had once been as familiar as Jolie's own. Hannah, with diamonds in her ears, and wearing a gown of midnight blue. Hannah, with her eyes red rimmed from crying.

'Why him?' said Hannah in a choked and bitter voice. 'You could have anyone you want. Anyone! All you've ever had to do was look their way. Couldn't you at least have had the decency to stay away from *him*?'

'You think I didn't try?' said Jolie. 'You think I wanted to fall for a man who would bring me back to this? A room full of people who think I'm a whore, and to you, who've hated me for more years than I can count for something that was never my fault? What have I ever done to you, Hannah?' It was a cry that went way back in time and it brought fresh tears to Hannah's eyes. 'What have I ever done *wrong*?'

'I *had* to choose,' raged the mirror person with the tears in her eyes. 'She *made* me choose, and now she's going to make me choose again. Because Cole looked at you and you looked back. Couldn't you have just gone and never looked back?'

'I tried,' said Jolie again. 'Hannah, I tried, and Cole came after me and he's good for me, and I'm good for him, and what we have together, it's so very bright and strong. It blinds me, Han. It blinds us both. All we're asking for is a chance to explore what's between us. Is that really so much to ask? I'm not a bad person. You *know* me. Am I really so wrong for him?'

'You don't know what you're up against,' said Hannah, fresh tears forming fast. 'There's nothing good left in my mother, Jolie. Nothing but bitterness and hate. You have no idea how easily she hates. It comes of being put last all the time in my father's affections; behind his precious company and his precious Rachel, and plenty else. It stems from twelve years' worth of putting up with those supercilious hags out there demeaning her every chance they got because she couldn't satisfy her husband. You think you're having a bad night out there? Do you really think this is as bad as it gets? Because it's not. It's going to get worse, a lot worse, and you're already hiding in the bathroom.'

'So are you,' said Jolie quietly. 'Why should you hide? Aren't you getting exactly what you want? Me being crucified out there?'

'He hasn't told you, has he? You don't even know what's really happening out there tonight. You're too busy wondering what people think of you,' said Hannah, with an icy laugh that echoed around the tiles. 'Well, let me give you the gift of clarity. Cole's out there fighting for control of the company tonight, Jolie. My mother's bringing a vote of no confidence against him. He's risking everything he's ever worked for.'

'And tearing our family apart.

'For you.'

CHAPTER TEN

HANNAH left. Jolie stayed, looking blindly in the mirror. A simple work dinner, Cole had said. Just the next step in our relationship. Not a test. Don't think of it as a test.

I'm not ready, she'd said, and she hadn't been. Not for this. The stakes were too high. The relationship was too new. And Jolie was too scared of the things Cole was willing to do for the right to simply be with her and see where this relationship would go.

Jolie touched up her make-up and reapplied her lipstick with an unsteady hand. She walked back down to the bar, only the bar was now empty and a waiter stood waiting to direct her to the function room.

Jolie looked at the door to the outside world and the urge to flee was overwhelming. Retreat, just retreat back into a world of fantasy and pictures. A world where reality simply didn't exist.

Reality was overrated.

'The gentleman said to direct you this way,' murmured the polite waiter, and gestured with his hands and offered up an encouraging smile, and Jolie made the mistake of looking in the direction he pointed and there stood Cole. A strong and beautiful man with forest-green eyes, hair the colour of charcoal and wings for those who could see them.

How could she simply walk away and leave him standing there? He deserved better than that from her. He deserved better from everyone.

Jolie began walking towards Cole. She smiled when she reached him, and let her eyes reveal how much she liked what she saw, and he returned the favour and for a moment it was just the two of them.

How she wished it were just the two of them.

He offered his arm and she took it and walked into the room beside him with her head held high, and, yes, it was a mask but it stuck and it hid her terror and it was the best she could do. Cole seated her at the end of the long banquet table and took the chair opposite her. Hannah was nowhere in sight.

'Where's Hannah?' she asked quietly.

'Hannah wasn't feeling well,' said the granite-eyed man who'd arrived with Hannah earlier in the evening. He took the seat next to Cole. 'She sends her apologies.'

'Jolie, this is Derek Haynes, my Deputy Executive Director. Derek, Jolie,' said Cole, making it swift and giving her no clue as to the other man's allegiance. And then the pregnant woman waddled up and sank into the seat next to Jolie. 'And this is Susan Price, executive PA to both Derek and me.'

Susan smiled at Jolie, seemingly without malice. 'I won money on you,' said Susan. 'And before it gets awkward, the baby's father is no longer in the picture and nor am I married. I prefer to think of this as proof that I *do* have a brain, even if I *did* temporarily misplace it.'

'Susan's a big fan of getting straight to the point and making herself brutally clear,' said Cole dryly. 'It's very useful at times.' And to Susan, 'Who did you speak to?'

'Max Cato is yours. Simon Pell's yours. Rufus is Christina's, and Jasper's hedging. Best call him Christina's.'

Warhammer guy, who was sitting on the other side of Susan, asked Susan if she'd like some water, and when she said yes he filled her glass from the carafe, and then those of the other people around him. Susan fell into conversation with them, giving Jolie the opportunity to conduct a semi-private conversation with Cole, give or take granite-eyed Derek listening in.

'Are these votes you're counting?' she asked Cole quietly.

'Not necessarily.'

'Because Hannah told me about your mother's plan to strip you of Rees Holdings,' said Jolie next.

'Hannah exaggerates,' said Cole.

'She didn't sound like she was exaggerating to me,' said Jolie, trying to smile. 'Three months ago I had a perfectly decent and useful existence. Manageable self-doubt. No big business or ugly social politics anywhere on my horizon. And then came you.'

'You can thank me later.'

'Right now I don't feel like thanking you at all.'

'It takes two, Red,' he said quietly.

'I know.'

The dinner went on for ever; at least that was how it felt to Jolie. Reality had it ending at a little after ten. Derek was still an unknown quantity although his allegiance was clearly to Cole. Susan was a treasure.

Warhammer guy's name was Mark. And Jasper wanted
Cole to send him the quarterly report—which apparently
wasn't due for another two weeks. Cole could send it
through tonight or tomorrow morning, he could send
it through incomplete, but one way or another Jasper
wanted it before the board meeting on Monday. Jasper
also suggested Cole send the report out to all the other
board members too.

It seemed to Jolie that Jasper didn't give a toss who
Jolie was or why Christina objected to her.

The elderly Jasper—who Cole said had been on the
board since Cole's grandfather had first founded it—
cared only for the well-being of the company.

'All-nighter at your place?' asked Derek once Jasper
had made his request and walked away.

Cole nodded. 'Jolie…it's not quite the way I'd planned
to end the evening, but would you mind?'

'I don't mind.'

'We're going to need Hannah there too,' said Derek,
with a quick glance in Jolie's direction. 'I'll go get
her.'

'Tell her—' Jolie wished there were some other way
to do this. Less public. Less choking. 'Tell her I won't
be there.'

'Stay,' said Cole later that evening, pulling things out of
Jolie's overnight bag just as fast as she could stuff them
in. 'We can work through this.'

'No, we can't. I know you think you can wear your
family down and get them to accept me, but it's not
going to happen, Cole. And I won't have you losing
everything because of me. It's time to finish this.'

More items went into her bag.

And came straight back out.

'I need you here,' he said gruffly.

'No, you need Derek here and Hannah here, and you need to get that report done.'

'Why are you being such a martyr? Because my mother's hurt that I'm seeing you? She *made* her bed, Jolie. And everyone around her had to lie in it. She should have let my father go. At least then she might have had a chance at happiness.'

'I agree with you,' said Jolie evenly. 'One hundred per cent I agree with you. Your mother didn't know when to let go. I do.'

'I will not be blackmailed into giving you up,' he roared.

'Then do it for me,' she shouted back. 'Because I can't live in that world you took me to tonight, Cole. With all its petty games and snide remarks, and Shakespeare quotes and clammy hands. *I won't live my life like that!'*

'Then *don't*! Doesn't mean you have to walk out on *me*. I have heard of compromise, Jolie. I do it every goddamn day! I'm asking you to believe in me. You have to believe that I can steer us through this.'

'Compromise? Cole, please!' Jolie laced her words with disbelief. 'You don't know the meaning of the word. You want what you want and you take it. Right or wrong you wanted me at that dinner tonight so you forced it. I'm standing here trying to pack my bag and you're standing there unpacking it. You're not *listening* to what the people around you are saying. How is that compromise? How is that any different from your father taking a mistress and to hell with the feelings of the people around him?'

'*I am not my father,*' he said, hot temper riding him hard.

'*Then stop acting like him!*' Temper lit her too, and fed her resolve. 'When are you going to learn that you can't always have what you want? That sometimes the cost is too high. That you don't *get* to call all the shots when it comes to continuing a relationship? I'm not strong enough for this battle, Cole. I'm telling you I can't walk in your world without losing every scrap of confidence I've ever had. I'm telling you I've been fighting your family's disapproval my entire life and I'm tired of it, Cole. I'm so tired of that fight.' Tears tracking down her face now, hot and stinging.

'I'll walk away,' he said huskily. 'From Rees Holdings. From my family. If that's what it takes to make you happy, I'll do it.'

'But it wouldn't make me happy, don't you see? I'm not worth that kind of sacrifice.'

'You are to me.'

'I've loved spending time with you,' she said huskily. 'I've enjoyed getting to know you, but there are things about you that scare me. Your strength of will. Your ruthlessness.'

'You're a match for them, Red. You're not so different yourself.'

'I don't love you.' It was a lie, the cruellest lie she'd ever told. Her next words were even crueller but she said them because without them he wouldn't let her go. 'I looked at you tonight and I didn't love what I saw. I saw James.'

And this time Cole shook his head and turned away and Jolie closed her eyes and wished herself in hell because surely hell was better than here.

'Go,' he said raggedly. 'Just go.'

He left the room and she finished packing. She called a taxi. She shouldered her bag and put her head down and headed for the door to Cole's house where Cole stood waiting, his lips tight and his eyes bleak.

'Was any of it real?' he said as she drew level with him, and put her hand to the doorknob. 'Or were you always aiming to make me fall in love with you so that you could finally take your revenge on the son for the sins of the father? Tell me, Red. I'd really like to know.' Jolie glanced his way and wished she hadn't, for his eyes flayed her more than words ever could. 'Were you always planning to walk away from me at the worst possible moment?'

CHAPTER ELEVEN

'I'M SET up on the dining-room table,' said Cole evenly when Derek and Hannah arrived some half an hour later. He'd had a shower. He'd buried his rage, his pain and his heartache for dealing with later. 'There's drip coffee in the pot, extension cords for your computers, and I'm pretty sure there's cake around here somewhere. Raspberry cakes and half a something or other from last night.'

Last night when the world had still been sane and Jolie had slept in his arms.

Hannah headed for the dining table and began unloading her laptop. Derek shoved his laptop and case on the kitchen counter and headed for the coffee. Cole headed for his sister, the one who wouldn't meet his gaze.

'She's not here, Han. Her choice, not mine, so here's what we're going to do. We're going to get the quarterly report done and sent out tonight. We're going to work up a business plan and we're going to talk through it at the board meeting on Monday. And if Christina raises a vote of no confidence against me and the pair of you vote together to bring me down, I'm going to propose that you take over Rees Holdings and I'm going to give you my proxy vote. It'll give you the block you need to bring the board to heel.'

'And then what?' Finally Hannah met his gaze, her eyes shocked and dark with pain.

'Then you run the company.' Cole tried to smile but found that he couldn't. 'Make it grow.'

'But what are *you* going to do?'

'Exactly what you think I'm going to do,' he said, and Hannah flinched and Cole drew her into his arms and she broke on his chest, her sobs loud and gulping. 'I will always love you,' he muttered into her hair. 'I will never turn you away; I need you to know that. And maybe I am like Dad in that I tried to force upon you a situation that neither you or our mother or Jolie were capable of handling. I saw only one way forwards and I rushed it and ignored the feelings of others, and I'm sorry for that, I really am. But for all that I'm like Dad in some ways, in others I'm not. I won't be blackmailed into giving Jolie up for the good of the company. I refuse to let Christina's bitterness rule my life. I'm not Dad, and I am done with being compared to him and I have finished paying for his mistakes. I'm going after her, Han. As soon as the meeting's over, and I don't know if she'll have me, and chances are she won't, but I have to try.'

'I hate you for this.'

'No, you don't,' he murmured.

'I hate Jolie too.'

'No, you don't,' he whispered again. 'You never have. You just hated having to push her away.'

Jolie arrived home on Sunday morning at around ten a.m. She'd stayed the night in a motel and had lucked a seat on the first flight to Christchurch the following morning. Arriving home didn't bring Jolie the tranquillity she craved. She'd brought the real world with her this time and there were still things she had to do in it before she could truly escape. A phone call, or two, to salvage what she could. For Cole.

This much she could do for him.

She dialled the first number. Christina Rees answered.

'Mrs Rees, it's been a long time since we last spoke.' A very long time, for Jolie had been only a kid at the time. Twelve years old and blissfully unaware of her mother's affair with Hannah's father. 'This is Jolie Tanner.' Jolie Tanner whose knees were shaking but whose voice was firm.

Christina Rees remained silent.

'I wish you could have been at the dinner last night,' said Jolie next. 'I think if we'd stood together against those black-hearted company wives you call your friends we could have stripped them of their power to hurt us and we could have both moved on. Somehow I always pictured you as the instigator of their malice rather than a victim and I'm sorry I misread that, I really am. I thought you were the strong one. I've always pictured you as strong.'

'Go away,' said Christina Rees. 'Why can't you just go *away*?'

'I did,' said Jolie. 'I got as far away from Queenstown as I could. And then your husband's death brought me back to comfort my mother, and I got stuck in a ski gondola with your son. I never set out to hurt you. I never set out to hurt anyone, but I did. Finally *I* did something that I knew was going to hurt you and I'm sorry for that. Please, Mrs Rees,' said Jolie raggedly. 'I'm gone now. I'm back in Christchurch and I won't be seeing Cole again and I want you to stop what you're doing to him and to Hannah, because you're tearing your family apart and I can't stand to watch. Surely there's more to you than bitterness and hate. There's grace in you too, and love for your children. Isn't there? Please, Mrs Rees, please stop what you're doing. I'm gone now. And I won't be coming back.'

'I wish I could believe you,' whispered Christina Rees, and then the phone went dead.

Christina Rees had hung up.

The next phone call Jolie made was to her mother. Rachel had never been blameless, when it came to her affair with James. She'd never pretended to be.

'The dinner didn't go so well,' said Jolie without pre-amble. 'I didn't fit in. The past happened. Forgiveness didn't happen. And now Christina Rees is going to try and take Rees Holdings away from Cole because he looked at me. Because I looked back. I came home. I called Christina Rees and told her I was out of Cole's life. I don't think she believed me.'

Rachel said nothing.

'Cole plans to fight her. At a board meeting on Monday morning, but I don't know how strong his po-sition is. I know Silverlake was underinsured. I know Cole's in the process of restructuring to make up the shortfall. I know the company's losing a lot of money right now, because of the loss of Silverlake income and because Cole kept so many Silverlake employees on the payroll. He's a good man. I wish...' Jolie closed her eyes. 'I wish you'd never done it, Mama. I wish all three of you had been stronger and more sensible and more *careful* of the hurt you inflicted on each other. Because someone has to pay for it, someone always has to pay, and right now those someones are Cole, and Hannah, and me.'

The quarterly report went out to the board of directors at seven-fifteen on Sunday morning. At eight forty-five Cole fielded his first phone call. At five forty-two that afternoon, a business strategy plan went out. At seven-fifteen that evening Cole turned off his phone and fell face down on his bed. Derek and Hannah had stayed to the end. Cole wanted Hannah fully informed on all aspects of Rees management, and as for Derek, he was the best asset Cole could give his sister if she did have to take up the company reins.

Cole hadn't asked Hannah which way she would throw her vote. Hannah hadn't said.

The only thing she had urged him to do as she was leaving, and Derek was leaving, was to go and see their mother and *talk* to her about his feelings and his hopes.

But Cole just shook his head.

'What am I going to say to her, Han? "Don't do this"?'

But Hannah's words kept worrying away in his brain, and finally he picked up his phone and dialled home. His mother didn't pick up so he left her a message.

'Mother, it's Cole. I just want to say that I know you're hurting right now, and that you have been for a long time. I had hoped that with Dad gone you might have been able to get on with your life. Forgive and forget. Something like that. But I guess not.'

Cole took a deep breath.

'I won't give Jolie up for you. I'm not Dad, I'm your son. I'm your son and I've finally found a woman I can love, and I deserve better from you than an ultimatum to give her up or lose the company. You didn't even give her a chance. That's what cuts at me the most. You never see past your own agenda to the hurt you inflict on the people around you. Someone accused me of doing the same this weekend and it cruelled me, but then I realised that when it came to my dealings with you in particular she was right. I have finally stopped caring whether I hurt you or not. You should probably take that as a warning.'

And with nothing left to say, Cole hung up.

He called Jolie next but she wasn't answering her phone, either. The words they'd exchanged last night had left him gutted. He had some answers for her, but not all. He had apologies to make and he didn't know where to start.

'Hey,' he murmured into her message bank, with the phone to his ear and his body splayed out on the bed. 'We pulled an all-nighter last night and worked all day through, but the quarterly's done, there's a strategy plan in place, a board meeting starting at nine tomorrow morning, and with or without me Rees Holdings is going to be fine. You seemed concerned about that and I just wanted you to know that there's no need to be.' That was the first part of the message and he got through it well enough. Now for the rest.

'You accused me of not listening to the people around me and of forcing you into a situation you weren't ready for, and not giving enough credence to your shyness, and I'm sorry for that. I'm listening now, so if you have anything more to say... I'm listening.'

He waited a breath, heartsick and exhausted. 'You accused me of being ruthless and to some extent you're right. I *am* being ruthless in not letting my mother's bitterness and hate colour my life. I make no apology for that. But I'm not always ruthless and I'm nowhere near as emotionally selfish as my father. *God*, that hurt, Red; when you said you looked at me and saw him, because I've spent the best part of my life doing my damnedest *not* to be like him. God help me, I am my own person.'

What else? What else did he have to say to the woman who held his heart so tightly? 'Compromise. I can do that. I'm an expert.'

What else? 'Stubborn, yes. I haven't given up on us. I can't. Not yet. I think back on the time we spent together and I *know* you weren't playing me. That you felt something for me.'

What else? 'Trust. Do you know how hard it is to trust people with a background like mine? Everyone wants something. Money, influence, support, a way of twisting the knife. Even my family—they're experts at twisting love and loyalty to their own purpose. Even Hannah. I love her, but I can't trust her. Do you know how long I've been looking for a woman I can trust? I thought I'd found her, Red. In you.'

Sleep, he had to get some sleep. He was hardly making sense, even to himself. 'I wish you hadn't run... I know how resilient you can be. I saw it on the mountain and in the way you pursued an artistic career. You never gave up. Not until the other night when you pushed me away and ran.' A shudder racked him, his body finally surrendering to despair. 'Why did you have to run?'

He ended the call and dropped the phone to the floor.

And he slept the sleep of the innocent and the damned.

Monday morning was one of those bright icy days winter delivered up so well. Cole took his seat at the head of the boardroom table with a calm he was far from feeling. The quarterly report showed Rees Holdings bleeding money. The business strategy plan that he, Hannah and Derek had worked so hard to finish and send out in advance of the meeting was a bold one and probably not what his father would have done.

Didn't mean it wasn't a sound strategy for digging themselves out of debt and putting them on a secure footing to move forward again. He was open to negotiation on some points. He wanted Jasper's input. Rufus's input he trusted less. Christina's not at all. Max and Simon were not present and only minor shareholders anyway, but they'd given their proxies to Cole.

He'd been through it all with Hannah.

Hannah had agreed.

Nothing to do now but declare the meeting open and see what came his way.

Christina's motion of no confidence in him came hot on the heels of the tabling of the quarterly report. She pointed to the bottom line and, yes, it was vividly red. An avalanche and the underinsuring of Silverlake had seen to that.

She pointed to various other problems within the

company that Cole hadn't known she was aware of. She never looked at him once.

'I find it hard to believe, Christina,' drawled Jasper, 'that you intend to blame the current bottom line on Cole's inability to manage Rees Holdings. Particularly when you know as well as I do whose signature was on the Silverlake insurance policy.'

'James was ill,' said Christina curtly. 'Cole should have checked it.'

'I dare say he would have,' said Jasper silkily, 'had James been inclined to let him. Cole didn't take full control of Rees Holdings until *after* James's death, Christina. Something to remember.'

Rufus seconded Christina's no confidence motion.

Jasper just closed his eyes.

'Hannah?' said Christina sharply, and for a moment Hannah appeared to crumple. It didn't matter, Cole told himself savagely. It didn't matter if Hannah voted against him too. The company was still secure, still safe from his mother's machinations.

Cole's gaze met Hannah's tortured one and he gave a tiny shrug. He'd promised himself he wouldn't get upset. People made choices, that was all. Choices they then had to live with. He'd already made his when it came to cutting his mother out of his life.

'Hannah,' said their mother again, and this time Hannah replied.

'You didn't even *look* at the strategy plan Cole sent through yesterday, did you, Mother?' said his sister flatly. 'You don't care what happens to the company. All you want to do is punish Cole because he won't stop seeing Jolie Tanner.'

Christina's lips pinched to white, but Hannah hadn't finished yet.

'Why can't you leave the past behind?' whispered Hannah. 'Why do you always have to be such a *victim*? The wronged wife. The wounded parent. Why must you always define yourself in relation to *him*? Daddy's *dead*. And yet even from the grave he's still pulling your strings so that every decision you make is nothing more than a knee-jerk reaction to some gutless decision of his. Can't you see *past* him for once? Can't you see past your own hurts to the damage you're doing?'

'Hannah, not here,' murmured Cole.

'Why *not* here? She brought it here. All our dirty laundry, all her bitterness and vengeance. I've listened to you and Derek and her all weekend long. Now it's time for you to listen to me. Cole, you have my full support when it comes to the running of this company. Between us we hold sixty per cent of the vote so I believe that settles the matter of no confidence. Mother, I'm sorry if you see this as a betrayal of your feelings but what you're doing here is wrong. Wrong for the company. Not fair to Cole. And not fair to me. Get over the past. That or get out of our lives. So…moving on.'

Hannah plucked the strategy plan from the papers stacked in front of her and held it up for all to see. 'Is anyone ready to discuss the plan for rescuing this company now? I for one would like to be out of here by five.'

Jolie got Cole's message Monday morning and played it twice and went to work and passed the day in a creative frenzy that didn't stop when she got home. She had paper and pencils at the ready and longing to put on the page.

Loss to put on the page too, along with other emotions she hadn't yet defined. She would discover them in the drawing of them. And then she would be able to return Cole's phone call and know what to say. That was the way it worked for Jolie. Always had.

A fizzy water, soon forgotten.

Textured paper, thick and ragged edged—her very best and to hell with the cost. Her favourite charcoals and a heart full of emotion. Her mind full of Cole, Jolie began to draw.

A slip of a girl in ripped denim and a shabby T-shirt lying barefoot and stomach down atop an icy glacier peak, one hand extended towards a climbing warrior, who wore skin-hugging breeches, and a belt from which all manner of swords and hammers hung.

The warrior's back was a study in strength and beauty and he was almost in reach of the waif's outstretched hand. A storm swirled all around them and colour was needed, blacks and blues wrapped in menacing greys. This picture she called Trust.

A slip of a girl in a warrior's embrace, and her face shone with wonder and passion and joy. This one she called Discovery.

A slip of a girl atop an icy mountain peak, with her head to her knees and her hands to her head while all around her winged demons rode the wind. The warrior fought them, he fought them with everything he had, his face a hard mask of determination even though he was outnumbered. Jolie hated this picture because the girl in it was a coward. She tossed it aside and started again, but no matter how she drew it the warrior remained steadfast and the girl refused to stand with him against their enemies.

Jolie started again, on a new series concerning the warrior, only this time he had two women flanking him and the girl tried to join them but the women wouldn't accept her so the girl just slunk away.

Jolie hated this series too. Coward, she called it.

At some stage during the evening she drew a series of lovers so lost in each other and composed of such beautiful lines and shadows that she started to weep. This one was Love and she'd lived every line of it.

She plastered the pictures around the living room wall, all of them, finished or not, and she tried to put them in order and she tried to draw the finish of it all and finally she put on paper a warrior triumphant, with his back towards the viewer so that she wouldn't have to draw his face.

The slip of a girl was nowhere to be seen.

Jolie had run out of charcoal and 6B pencils.

She hadn't run out of tears.

She started again with more paper and pastels and this time she drew a room full of beautiful people and the slip of a girl was amongst them. The girl looked the part and the girl was not alone. The warrior stood near her only this time he wore a suit, and he looked at the girl with pride and she smiled back at him with pleasure and her heart was full of love. The colours on the paper grew richer as Jolie worked, the faces of the people in the crowd grew more vivid but the connection and the trust between the warrior and the waif remained secure.

Jolie liked this one.

She found her fizzy water and sat on the couch and stared at it for a very long time.

She could have done it. Despite the ugly in Saturday

night's dinner with Cole's colleagues, parts of the evening had worked. Given time, and Cole's support, she could have walked in that world when required. Compromise, she called it. Such a tiny price to pay in the name of Love.

What had happened today with her snow-kissed warrior? Had he fought his mother for control of the company? Had he won?

Jolie stared hard at the last picture she'd taped to the wall of the Victory Warrior. She wanted so badly to be in it. Standing there next to her warrior having *fought* for that right.

But she hadn't fought, she'd run away instead.

A coward and a fool.

Jolie closed her eyes and wished herself away. 'I'm listening,' he'd said in the message she had yet to reply to. 'I'm listening now, so if you have anything more to say…'

Reaching for a new sheet of paper Jolie clipped it to her easel and started to draw.

Cole Rees, CEO of Rees Holdings, parked his hire car in the almost deserted car park across the road from the shabby block of Christchurch flats and steeled himself for the walk across the way and up the stairs to Jolie's door. He'd come because he couldn't not come. He'd come bearing gifts and words, and he'd come to bare his heart, even if Jolie's words had not changed.

'I don't love you,' she'd said. 'I've loved spending time with you. I've enjoyed getting to know you. I don't love you. I looked at you tonight and I didn't love what I saw. I saw James.'

Maybe Cole loved unwisely, as his father had done,

but love he did and pursue Jolie he would until she told him again and broke his heart for certain. She knew the words. She'd said them two days ago.

'I can't walk in your world.... I don't love you.'

Light shone from Jolie's kitchen window. Jolie was home; that was the good news.

But she hadn't returned his call.

Resolutely, Cole picked up his gifts and started forward with feet of lead and fear skidding down his spine the likes of which he'd never known. 'You can do this,' he murmured. 'You know how this goes. Just put one foot in front of the other and climb.'

When the doorbell rang it took some time before Jolie registered the noise. She had music playing. She wasn't expecting anyone. She hadn't finished drawing and didn't want the interruption. But she went to the door and she asked who it was, and when the person on the other side answered she opened the door and stared.

'Hey, Red,' he said quietly, and Jolie blinked back sudden tears. 'You didn't return my call, and I figured you might want to know what happened at the meeting today. Hannah stood by me. The company's still mine, such as it is. Your mother gave me sixteen million pounds' worth of shares I have no idea what to do with. I'm thinking of putting them in the too-hard basket for a while and then giving them to you.'

'I won't thank you,' she murmured.

'I know. That's the beauty of it.' He stood there in her doorway, a snow-kissed man with questions in his eyes. 'May I come in?'

So she stood aside, and let him enter, and watched

him come to a halt not two steps into the room. He stared at the walls. At the drawings she'd stuck all over them.

'Oh, Red,' he murmured. 'What's going on?'

'I'm thinking,' she said, and her words came out on a sob. 'I couldn't think. I'm so sorry I left you the other night. I'm a coward. A coward and a fool and I know it, and I love you, and I don't know what to do. I'm thinking.' She gestured towards the walls. 'This is how I think, and now you're going to think I'm mad as well as being a coward and a fool.'

'Wait here,' he said. 'Just wait.' And he went back to the door and bent down to pick something up off the floor outside and when he turned round he had champagne and roses in his hands, and he handed them to her, and shut the door behind him. 'So, I thought about what it was that Jolie Tanner might want,' he said gruffly. 'And I came up with those and I came here with this.'

He pulled a black velvet ring box from his overcoat pocket and held it out towards her. 'Champagne and roses and a loving partner for Jolie Tanner. Someone who's proud of her and supportive of her, and who knows that she's shy and connects deeply with her art and doesn't always deal perfectly with reality, but then who does? Someone who loves her for exactly who she is and doesn't give a damn what other people think or say. I hope I got it right.'

'You did,' she whispered, and her vision blurred.

'Open the box, Red.'

Jolie set Cole's other gifts aside. The velvet box felt soft against her fingertips. The solitaire diamond engagement ring that nestled inside it blazed brighter than any star in the sky.

'Now you put it on,' he murmured.

'You're getting very dictatorial.'

'I've had a hard day. Marry me, Jolie. Please. You're not a coward. I put you in an impossible situation, but it's fixed now and I need you at my side. I've seen you take on a mountain and win. We can do this. You just have to want to.'

'I do want to,' she whispered and stepped joyously into his embrace, still clutching the little velvet box in her hands. She hadn't put the ring on yet but she would, she most certainly would. 'I'm getting charcoal all over your fancy suit.' Charcoal and tears.

'I want charcoal all over my fancy suit,' he said, and with a glance at the half-drawn picture gracing the easel, a picture of a warrior fine lost in the arms of the waif who loved him, 'I also want wings.'

'You don't need wings,' she murmured. 'You already walk on water.'

'Yeah, but I want the sky, as well.'

'Greedy,' she said, and pulled back just a little to study him. 'I love you,' she murmured and kissed him once. 'I'll marry you, and stand by you. Fight for you. Fight with you, when I have to. We can do this.'

'I know,' he said, and his hand came up to cup her cheek, slow and warm and easy. Such an easy touch for such a complex and courageous man. 'It's just another mountain, love.'

Harlequin *Presents*

Coming Next Month

from **Harlequin Presents®**. Available August 30, 2011

Coming Next Month

from **Harlequin Presents® EXTRA**. Available September 13, 2011

**Visit www.HarlequinInsideRomance.com
for more information on upcoming titles!**

REQUEST YOUR FREE BOOKS!

New York Times *and* USA TODAY *bestselling author*
Maya Banks presents a brand-new miniseries

PREGNANCY & PASSION

*When four irresistible tycoons face
the consequences of temptation.*

Book 1—ENTICED BY HIS FORGOTTEN LOVER

Available September 2011 from Harlequin® Desire®!

Rafael de Luca had been in bad situations before. A crowded ballroom could never make him sweat.

These people would never know that he had no memory of any of them.

He surveyed the party with grim tolerance, searching for the source of his unease.

At first his gaze flickered past her, but he yanked his attention back to a woman across the room. Her stare bored holes through him. Unflinching and steady, even when his eyes locked with hers.

Petite, even in heels, she had a creamy olive complexion. A wealth of inky-black curls cascaded over her shoulders and her eyes were equally dark.

She looked at him as if she'd already judged him and found him lacking. He'd never seen her before in his life. Or had he?

He cursed the gaping hole in his memory. He'd been diagnosed with selective amnesia after his accident four months ago. Which seemed like complete and utter bull. No one got amnesia except hysterical women in bad soap operas.

With a smile, he disengaged himself from the group

around him and made his way to the mystery woman.

She wasn't coy. She stared straight at him as he approached, her chin thrust upward in defiance.

"Excuse me, but have we met?" he asked in his smoothest voice.

His gaze moved over the generous swell of her breasts pushed up by the empire waist of her black cocktail dress.

When he glanced back up at her face, he saw fury in her eyes.

"Have we *met?*" Her voice was barely a whisper, but he felt each word like the crack of a whip.

Before he could process her response, she nailed him with a right hook. He stumbled back, holding his nose.

One of his guards stepped between Rafe and the woman, accidentally sending her to one knee. Her hand flew to the folds of her dress.

It was then, as she cupped her belly, that the realization hit him. She was pregnant.

Her eyes flashing, she turned and ran down the marble hallway.

Rafael ran after her. He burst from the hotel lobby, and saw two shoes sparkling in the moonlight, twinkling at him.

He blew out his breath in frustration and then shoved the pair of sparkly, ultrafeminine heels at his head of security.

"Find the woman who wore these shoes."

Will Rafael find his mystery woman?
Find out in Maya Banks's passionate new novel
ENTICED BY HIS FORGOTTEN LOVER
Available September 2011 from Harlequin® Desire®!